Original title: *Messer Arcibaldo. Lettere di un esperto diavolo a un apprendista tentatore*

© 2021 Fede & Cultura, Verona, Italy

Translated into English by Karen Darantière

English edition © 2024 Voice of the Family, Calx Mariae Publishing

Calx Mariae Publishing is an imprint of Voice of the Family, London, United Kingdom.

ISBN: 978-1-8384785-7-5

www.voiceofthefamily.com

TABLE OF CONTENTS

The humans live in time but our Enemy destines them to eternity. He therefore, I believe, wants them to attend chiefly to two things, to eternity itself, and to that point of time which they call the Present. For the Present is the point at which time touches eternity.

C.S. Lewis, *The Screwtape Letters*

The devil, even if he is our enemy, can only overcome those who listen to him. He doesn't have the strength to coerce, only the cunning to flatter.

Saint Augustine, *Sermon 16B*

INTRODUCTION

I really cannot recall just *how* this correspondence happened
to fall into my hands. What I can say is that certain facts, too
uncanny to be of merely human origin, as well as certain
reflections of mine on our present time and on our way of
living the faith within the Church itself, have prompted me
to take an earnest interest in a recent series of letters which
a venerable master from the abyssal depths, the chief of staff
in charge of all major decisions, has written to one of his
young disciples, a novice tempter learning the tricks of the
trade. It is indeed a truly unique art: seducing men with their
own seductions, convincing them to be the protagonists of
a brand-new story, of a novel way of being Christian. And
yet, it is a path that many before us have trodden, inspired by
ideas of which the source is superior to the ideas themselves.
There is an original temptation that reappears from time to
time in every human life, coming from a voice that whispers
in our ears: "You will be like God if you heed my words,
which in fact tell you nothing other than what you yourself
desire: your own ego above all else, even above God, if He
ever existed in the first place."

A disobedience coming from afar threatens our obedience, regardless of whether we actually believe this voice
or not, whether we think these words true or false. Such is
the mystery we must grapple with and attempt to unravel.
A persuasive voice tantalises us in an attempt to ruin our lives

forever — forcing us, more often than not, to focus solely on ourselves, to envelop ourselves exclusively in worldly and temporal concerns.

It is the voice of His Infernal Highness Arcibaldo, who confides his secrets to his pupil Polliodoro, a promising young tempter freshly appointed to attend to human souls, and who teaches him the fine art of luring souls and keeping them on the wide and crooked path to perdition. Unsurprisingly, it is not always easy to understand when the devil is speaking in earnest or deceptively, as after all, he is known to be the father of lies (cf. Jn 8:44). Yet even *he* is forced to tell the truth once in a while, in spite of himself, because otherwise the young devil might not quite grasp his meaning, but above all because if he lied to himself and to those belonging to his kingdom, he would be divided against himself and his kingdom could not stand (cf. Lk 11:18). The more thoughtful and serious humans have learned from experience and throughout history that if his kingdom *does* stand, it is thanks to pride and patience, which alone allow it to rise up as an anti-kingdom and even an anti-Church.

But the devil too, like any other spiritual being, finds himself confronted with an insurmountable obstacle: in order to deny the truth, he must first affirm it, even unknowingly. If he stubbornly persists in denying his own denial — whoever is accustomed to denying everything doesn't hesitate to indulge in this pleasure when the opportunity arises — he is perpetually tormented by the sense that this lie which he himself has concocted is neither very effective nor persuasive. Sooner or later it ends up revealing itself as less than true, and the deception is brought to light.

Things have a habit, though sometimes only after some delay, of showing themselves for what they truly are: true or false, good or bad. But the evil one possesses a vice all his own. He is the only one who is unable to recognise things for what they are or to recognise *himself* for what he is, though he is capable of patient and tireless efforts to pass off what does not conform to reality as *his* and ultimately *my truth.* His subversive efforts could be summarised in this way: to make what is unimportant and perhaps even useless appear as necessary, and as useless and unimportant that which *is* necessary. And if, one day, it just so happens that the practical things of life impose themselves upon the indispensable ones of faith, boasting that they take precedence by reason of their existence — their *being* here and now — then we will certainly be faced with the manoeuvring of the (real) enemy.

Sometimes, however, it is Polliodoro who, with a pinch of pride and pedantry, poses as the master. He takes up pen and paper and turns to his teacher to inform him of some delicate situation that seems to risk ruining their hellish plan, or to vindicate himself by showing off some original analysis of his concerning the situations in which he finds himself. Maybe by doing this, he can impress his superior enough to get promoted. The lust of careerism also affects the spirits of the lower regions.

Peering into this very interesting correspondence, it became ever clearer to me that it was my duty to pay homage to a great Irish-born writer, who spent much of his life in Oxford and Cambridge, and to his masterpiece, *The Screwtape Letters: Letters from a Senior to a Junior Devil*. Clive Staples Lewis (1898–1963) was the first to show interest in infernal correspondences and action plans from the dregs of the eternal underworld.

The following letters are my attempt to emulate this epistolary masterpiece. I have the highest regard for the lucidity of his judgements, and for his dry English humour, which he conveys through the arduous art of the ventriloquist (as he himself called it). Sometimes we sense that we already know what the devil thinks, simply because temptation almost always follows the same script. Yet it is not so easy to write a yes when you know it means *no*, or vice versa. This is complicated further still when this *yes* and *no*, or vice versa, is pronounced by some member of the Church or even the high-ranking clergy. The devil, not just any ordinary person, is a roaring lion who always prowls about looking for some prey to devour (cf. 1 Pt 5:8). Today it seems that this prey is not only easy to catch, but that it knows this and is even proud of the fact, or that in any case, it deceives itself by its own deeds.

An important fact that the reader will have to keep in mind is that in this correspondence, the art of tempting is not depicted as targeting any victim in particular, but rather the faith, the Church and our way of being Christians nowadays. It is a theological technique that borders on the "diabo-logical" or vice versa. It seems that the devil takes pleasure in seeing how the Church in her ministers, educated by the usual Arcibaldos, is being forced to play an insignificant role, and to become one day, in the not so distant future, irrelevant by virtue of the deeds of her own ministers. And this would constitute a diabolical victory only to be completed with a toast to a job impeccably well done. And yet His Infernal Highness Arcibaldo is never quite sure of himself, because some alert souls might just begin to open their eyes and see his seduction for what it is. Good will not give in so easily. However much it may be trampled upon, outraged, and mocked, it still endures for all to see. Evil can never claim the final victory, even if it is accompanied by all the hounds of hell, because it is always and only an opposition to good, and lasts only so long as there is someone willing to engage in this opposition. If good were to cease existing, this opposition would come to an end as well. And what is more, good alone is infinite. Evil is always and only finite.

C.S. Lewis wrote in his preface to *The Screwtape Letters* that there are two similar although complementary pitfalls into which one can fall when it comes to devils: either doubting their very existence or believing in them, but with an excessive interest — almost an obsession. The devils themselves delight in both and welcome a materialist as wholeheartedly as they do a magician. Their technique consists in convincing someone to be one or the other and then separating him from everyone else forever. Is it not true that the arts of the materialist and of the magician are back in fashion? Thus the devil's existence is denied by portraying him as a mere symbol of evil, or else, by attributing all man's misfortunes to him — including those of the Church — to the point of clouding the responsibility of men and of pastors. As St Augustine brilliantly said in one of his discourses (163B):

> "The devil must not be blamed in every instance; sometimes, in fact, man himself is a devil towards himself. So why must we beware of the devil? Precisely for this reason: so as not to deceive ourselves."

Nonetheless, one thing prompted me to pay close attention to this correspondence and to ensure that it was not lost. Above all, the devil and the priest do the same job: they go in search of souls. And both of them could, without difficulty, make their own the motto of St John Bosco: *Da mihi animas, cetera tolle* — "Give me souls and take away all the rest".

And so the time has come to take a look at this correspondence and to get to know that ancient craft, of which the practitioners have a predilection for the soul above all else: the soul, the real man as he is himself, who will be forever himself and cannot be confused with anyone else.

One last word to the wise reader. The names chosen do not correspond to any particular person. They are rather the free expression of a way of thinking which, by some strange coincidence, brings the world of mortals closer to that of the hereafter.

I.
Tactical preliminaries:
time and the world

Dear Polliodoro,

You must surely be wondering why you have received this letter from me. It is with great pleasure that I have learned that you have been selected by our profound Master from among your fellow classmates to begin a probation period at my school, under my guidance. By virtue of my vast experience, I have been given the mission of training you in the fine art of seducing souls, of leading them astray for all eternity and thus of conquering them for our kingdom, where darkness is light. Because, despite this darkness, there can be seen the shadows of many selves; each one reflecting the face of someone who wants to be only himself and not another, let alone an Other.

We must get to work at once, without wasting precious time. Time, as mortals say, is short; not for us, of course, who are not in time. However, even we must deal with its consequences. Our task of re-educating souls, according to the principles and norms of our mission, requires that everything be contemplated *sub specie damnationis* — that is, according to that most compelling cause of concern to us: the eternal damnation of men, and their being separated from the Enemy forever. Those self-deceiving theologians, charlatans of the divine, consider things and events *sub specie aeternitatis*. This is not our way of reasoning; never do we measure anything based on any such notion of time as opening onto eternity. And yet time is precious to us; it is the moment by which we can measure our work of saving man from himself and from the Enemy. Time is for us the very core of our action and, through time, we convince humans that it is better to waste it, before going on to lay waste to what is of the utmost importance: their own soul. Indeed, if they squander time, they are capable of doing the same to their soul, and being lost for all eternity; and so we will convince them that wasting time in this life, by carelessly and effortlessly letting themselves go with the flow of time, is essentially what man's journey is all about — his way of making progress. Man is like a ship which, ploughing through the sea, divides it into two opposing sides, almost like two irreconcilable enemies, but which are reunited as soon as the ship passes by, as if nothing had even happened. "Progress" will be our buzzword! After all, who is there that has no desire, nor any craving for it? Among those rare oddities who dub themselves "theologians" — such a distasteful word, as it contains a name so repugnant to us that the mere thought of it makes us nauseous — some even seek to measure their science according to this notion of "progress". So they judge it on the basis of whether or not (and how) it helps to bring about some change or other, or at the very least, *to initiate a process*.

Indeed, Polliodoro, you will need to keep firmly in mind that the best way to make man forget his eternal destiny is to distract him in this life, not so much by tempting him with frivolous pleasures or laxity regarding sins of the flesh — things to which he is naturally inclined without needing any assistance of ours — but rather by convincing him that his life is a mere journeying in time. A journey in his own existence, which he can observe, but always from the outside, like a spectator frozen in front of a television screen, or like those unable to wrench themselves from the screens of their mobile phones. Ah, what a great find that was! They are mesmerised by it, mere spectators of an existence that others are experiencing — perhaps that of the programmers of those applications — but no longer of themselves. They have no time to think, nor even to switch off the screen (whatever its size). First-rate results! We can truly take pride in such an outstanding outcome. Our aim is to fill their minds with this simple yet fitting concept: life is in time, time flows and therefore we flow with time. Such is life.

Indeed, ours is a very doctrinal way — how it makes me chuckle, attributing to ourselves a way of acting which is so remote from our way of being — a way that we snatch from the hands of the Enemy by distorting it; a way apparently more apprehensible but no less apt to seduce, with kid gloves as it were, artfully and delicately. We will claim that life is a *journey* and since men cannot help but journey on, one must let them travel ever onward, but only as aimless wanderers who never think about where they might be heading. We must distract them from thinking about their ultimate end, the very reason for which the Enemy has created them in the first place.

There is no better way to do this than to suggest to them that those who stop moving are lost. Let them go through time, furrow it and continue ceaselessly doing so, and sooner or later they will come to see time as the very essence of things, of the spirit, of the Enemy. We will reduce the Enemy to this notion of time, so that time will be *their* enemy, but *our* ally. We will make sure that they think that time alone exists, and no longer eternity, so that they will be ours forever, and they will have all eternity to experience the warmth of our company. Thanks to this eternity of time, we will teach them to forget the time of eternity.

Everything is to be judged on the basis of time. What a truly marvellous opportunity we have been given to seduce men into singing the praises not simply of the past but of time in and of itself. Time as it flows. Despite the fact that some of their "theologians" — from now on I will call them *sorcerers of sublime thought* so as to dispense with this unutterable word that evokes a grave matter, the science of the Enemy, but which fortunately we have largely succeeded in watering down — being more accustomed to abstruse thinking, say with Horace that man cannot be *laudator temporis acti* ("one who does nothing but praise the past"). Time is time! If it flows, it is not measurable and therefore, it matters not one whit whether it is past or present or yet to come. What matters is that it is what it is. Time and nothing more.

If we can then found all discussion upon this fluid connotation of time, without a single soul willing to enter time and stop it at its eternal present, the battle will have been won. The dimension of time will enter the mystery of the Enemy to the point of constituting His divine essence. Everything will begin to evolve. Faith, dogmas, the precepts of the Church. This theological system (which ought instead to aim at distinguishing in order to unite, so as to contemplate all the mysteries as an *unum*) will swallow itself up. It places something before their eyes only to take it away immediately. Contradiction will enter their faith and this faith will be a way to have a sort of certainty — you need not fret over any vain attempt to wrap your head round this abstruse nonsense — but it will no longer be what it is. At best it will become a palliative for pain relief, a good-mood pill that they take to cheer themselves up. Their faith will become our method for introducing the evolution of time into the doctrine, which is supposed to be revealed and immutable.

No need then for us to exhaust ourselves by the hard labour of making the believer lose his faith. Thanks to this new-fangled faith, with its historicist and evolutionist veneer, the believer will simply be someone who believes *in us*, because he will begin to believe more in himself, in the certainties derived from his own interpretative skills, or in his need for relief from the burden of existence. And he will forget that faith, as our adversaries claim, is a gift from on high, which descends from the eternity of the Enemy into the time of our patients. A soul steeped in time, with no thought of eternity, is a man who lives in a continuous and instantaneous extinction of his own existence, towards a never-ending underworld hereafter. This is precisely as we wish it to be. He will be our welcome guest — without even noticing it — simply by moving on, journeying in time. We will make him change his faith and moral perspective, but without much fanfare. And so we will finally be successful in rendering their Church insignificant. It will still remain visible but will no longer have much of anything to say. As the Church disappears, so does their Christianity. And ultimately, so does that Man-God Whose Name for us is unutterable.

My beloved and esteemed Polliodoro, I know just how talented and excellent you are, and that it is for this very reason that you have been chosen among many in your class. So be prepared to follow me as a dutiful disciple along this itinerary that I would define as diabo-logical. You know, of course that, by this expression, I am referring to our art of silent and persistent indoctrination, a reversal of their catechesis, of the unchanging catechism that our patients would like to teach to others so as to make more disciples. We have to prevent them from doing this. But I see, to my great satisfaction, that most of them have already seen to this. Following time and evolution, they are already saying that the catechism that was taught in past times is no longer good, that it has changed, that it changes with time. This is indeed what I call striking the right note! We only have to make sure that, in their formation sessions, the word "catechism" is understood to be a transmission of faith to be measured according to the time in which one lives, so that time becomes the measure of faith, and therefore faith is no longer the measure of life and of man. Have I made myself crystal clear? It is we who are the measure of time and life.

I have been told that at times you have been known to grow weary of learning, that you find it a bit fastidious to follow the most organic and logical reasoning. I can assure you, however, that at my school you will make great progress; you will be better trained than anywhere else, becoming a prize pupil and then a model master of seduction. You are a more pragmatic type, yet you have been chosen from among your companions in eternal misadventure due to your tenacity. I have heard that you are the most self-confident young tempter in your group, and I am aware that you have only recently joined us after a career that came to a premature end when you too, still in that dimension of time, were worthily deceived by those who suggested that religion changes according to fashions and interpretations, that it evolves, that the Enemy is both good and bad at once. Once the target, you have now become the shootist, and you may be proud of the fact … I beg your pardon, I should not have said "target", which would be to admit that we are capable of missing. We, most enlightened of all beings, never miss. We, wise instructors of humanity, lovers of our own good, know what it means to hate, but we do not know what it means to be wrong. We nearly always get it right. What distinguishes us is an iron will to teach everyone to hate in union with us forever, but without making mistakes. This is the true way to love. They will claim that we are failures, but on the contrary, our endeavours aim at illuminating their minds and extinguishing in them all thirst for truth and eternity.

Do you recall that passage from that sacred book, so hateful to us, which they call the Gospel, which says, "What does it profit a man if he gains the whole world, but loses his own soul? Or what can a man give in exchange for his soul?" (Mt 16:26) Well, we're going to turn it on its head and say, "What does it profit a man if he gains his soul, but loses the whole world? Or what can a man give in exchange for the whole world?" This will be our programme, our doctrine.

And if those on the opposing side, by using their intelligence and seeking divine assistance, understand this ruse and rid themselves of us by resorting to the Enemy, well, that's quite a different matter. Might we, in spite of ourselves, incite them to return to their God? Might we inadvertently be the instruments of their conversion and salvation? Maybe, but let us not trouble ourselves too much about that. We certainly cannot eliminate the risk that someone might notice our underhanded manoeuvring and consider us to be propitious messengers, permitting men to find the Enemy and get closer to Him. Anyway, all that is outdated stuff, old-school Catholic indoctrination. Even their sorcerers of sublime thought no longer believe in all that. All our skill must aim at this:

that many, many, souls notice nothing of all this, our artful craft. That is why we have to work hard, relentlessly. What counts is to proselytise. Our reputation as expert seducers of souls is at stake. Or perhaps, to put it better, as expert seducers of soulless bodies, as we have already robbed them of their very souls — incomprehensible souls, because they have remained enveloped and shrouded in time — of a faith without its doctrine, because they have been deceived by our scientific and truly diabo-logical knowledge. An alternative but highly convincing way of thinking it is indeed. So come, follow me and make sure you stay sharp and alert.

From the depths of hell, your very fond mentor,

II.
The obstacle

Dear Polliodoro,

As I told you in my previous letter, we must prepare ourselves well for each and every endeavour. Every good deed demands careful preparation. Naturally, we are not wanting in either intelligence or shrewdness. We are perhaps currently lacking a thorough and meticulous study of many of those "black holes" of Christianity, into which one can fall without knowing how one will get out, if ever one would succeed in getting out at all. Our adversaries call them mysteries, but we scoff at such nonsense. They are simply black holes, though I am afraid that not even our most penetrating darkness has been able to sound them out. One such hole is, so it seems to me, what they call *bonum* — "the good" — which is obviously what we rightly call evil. However, for the sake of brevity and clarity, I too will refer to it as "good". We will leave our beloved evil to its own devices for the time being while we attempt to put ourselves in our adversaries' shoes. Allow me to think aloud before we embark on this important mission. And don't give me any of that rubbish about just getting down to business, by acting straight away without due premeditation, prone as you are to one of your bouts of intellectual sloth. For let us not forget that acting follows being, even in our case. Thoughtless action would be the surest sign of recklessness on our part. And we could very well pay quite dearly for that.

It defies our comprehension most of the time, how it is that the good endures, constantly reappearing at the surface, always having an edge on evil and on our ability to get our work done properly; although weaker and easily overwhelmed, it resists, and sometimes — despite all our best efforts — it even comes out victorious. What is certain, above all, is that it will not die. We have not yet found a way to defeat it. And I regret to say that I do not think we will ever manage to do so. We know that the Enemy is more powerful than we are. He is the Good. I say this against my will, but I am forced to recognise it, otherwise I would be lying to myself and to you, my dear colleague of tenebrous misadventures. We are masters of lies, but only with regard to others. We deceive others, but we would never want to fall into the trap of an endless deception by deceiving ourselves also. That would be most unbearable for us, we who take so much pride in being free-thinkers. Let us tell each other the truth. And anyway, before Him we can only tell the truth and nothing but the truth.

However, He who is the Good, by binding the capacity to do good to the will of man and to his freedom, in a certain sense also binds His own omnipotence. When the good wins, He wins. And when it loses, He loses. We have our ways of ensuring that it does not win, of hindering the good and therefore of vanquishing it, and ultimately of vanquishing the Enemy Himself. Yet the good just will not back down. It is patient and humble. It is always lurking here, there and everywhere. Despite all the calamities that threaten to overcome it, despite all its ups and downs, it can always be found standing firmly at its post. However many insults and ignominies of all sorts it may suffer, though it may bend, it will not break. It simply will not retreat. Why is this so? Might this not end up being our ultimate downfall? Might we not one day see the good triumph by emerging, as it were, from a prolonged silence, from a merely apparent absence?

Come what may, we will carry on in our efforts to overcome the good by teaching men to ignore it altogether, by elevating ignorance to a programme of moral brainwashing, with much malice on our part. We are quite content to lead men along the royal road to damnation, for such is our vocation. Sometimes I take pride in referring to myself as a missionary of eternal unhappiness. It is a little pleasure of mine. A bitter sort of pleasure it is, since, in any case, it is intermingled with suffering. Deep down we know we have been defeated, but we cannot bring ourselves to admit it. It would only increase our already deep despair.

I cannot hide from you a slight fear of mine. Might we not one day be defeated once and for all by this patient perseverance of the good, by its unfailing endurance? Why is it that, even if torn to shreds by our relentless propaganda, this cursed good will not vanish from our sight? Though it suffers, it still hopes. We, on the other hand, suffer and despair. I am certainly not one to be all of a sudden struck by any longing for conversion. The mere thought of such a folly would be highly reprehensible. Yet how fascinating for us is that black hole of the good! We forge ahead in our mission of perverting mankind, convincing them not to give a fig about the good. Deep down, they know that being good is a weakness. They are fully aware that turning the other cheek, as their Master tells them, is neither pleasant nor natural; it is painful, even inhuman and abhorrent at times. Men spontaneously reject such weakness. However, at the end of the day, I have the inkling that it is precisely this weakness that makes the good so strong.

Shall we continue to tempt them? Most certainly. But we ought to expect some nasty surprises along the way; not a defeat for us or for our profound Master and the infernal legions who surround him — we would hear of no such thing — but perhaps a disappointment or two, like that of seeing more souls abandon our camp and join that of the Enemy. However hard it may be for us to admit, the good is still there, and the battle is still being waged. We will teach men to renounce the good, not to hold fast to it. To achieve this goal, we will never back down. My only fear is that some of them will persist in their obstinate refusal to give in.

The strategy that I proposed to you in my first letter is the most suitable one to ensure that, over time, men end up renouncing the good: we will let them drown in time; immersed as they are in its continual flow, they will become conscious of just how frail the good is, and they will be aware of little else. They will be incapable of perceiving how resilient the good is, because the time they have at their disposal will not permit this. They would need more time for reflection and for prayer. But teaching them to live for time and time alone is tantamount to denying them the time to reflect and to pray. They will say, after a short while, that the good is feeble, that it is easily overcome by evil. In the daily news, as in their daily lives, everything speaks of this fragility. As soon as we see them intent on discovering the causes, we will immediately counterattack by inspiring them with new and frivolous thoughts relating to the "good old days", or to a new day that is theirs to seize. We must never allow them to stop and think — let alone pray. "Don't be left behind, keep up with the times!" Such will be our motto to muddle their minds, making them lose any sense of goodness; such will be our winning strategy.

Without a doubt, alongside the task of convincing men that time is superior to being, and therefore to the good, we should always be equipped with another useful weapon: the seduction of pleasure. We will befuddle their minds so that they will search not for their true good but for a mere appearance thereof, namely, for pleasure. The longing for a good that satisfies the human appetite is always stronger than the search for the true good that requires effort, suffering, and penance, but which alone satisfies the soul, making man good. Pleasure is immediate, while the good is not. Pleasure comes cost-free, whereas the good does not. So why should they prefer the good to pleasure? Let us lure them with every imaginable pleasure! This is precisely why so many of them listen to us and follow us ever-downward.

Never forget, Polliodoro, that we are engaged in a wide-ranging and long-term endeavour to crack the toughest nuts: those who know how to renounce pleasures, but not the pleasure of the good, conquered after much effort and struggle. We must also persuade these souls to forget the good, by showing them firstly that there exists a rift between goodness and pleasure, and that the good, moreover, is unpleasant except when pursued for pleasure. We will tell them that they ought to focus first on the pleasure of the good before letting them savour the goodness of pleasure. And so pleasure alone will remain and no longer the good. They will be demoralised by defeat and the good will vanish from their horizon, being perceived as something arduous and perhaps even as a trap and a temptation.

Time and pleasure play a capital role in distracting men — especially the thinking heads among them — from the good. Here we have another opportunity to win over their sorcerers of sublime thought (or *of the sacred*, if you prefer). We must lead them all into temptation. The good is always difficult to conquer: this will be our trump card. The ancient sages (our adversaries) rightly said, *bonum ex integra causa, male ex quacumque defectu*. The good, in order for it to be such, requires an entirely righteous cause. Everything in an action must be good for the action to be good: the intention of the one choosing the action, the action being chosen and the end being sought. On the other hand, it does not take much to do evil; the least flaw ruins all.

In that horrid book of theirs that they call the Gospel (how unpleasant is the mere mention of it!) we read an enigmatic but significant sentence, which expresses a concept that is quite suitable for our purposes: "The kingdom of heaven suffers violence and the violent take it by force." (Mt 11:12) Have you got the gist of it? To be violent, it is necessary to fight, to resist the lure of evil and stand firmly in the good and thus gain the kingdom of heaven, as did that little fellow, so intransigent in dialogue, called St John the Baptist, to whom this passage refers. But who takes pleasure in doing violence to himself? Who likes getting hurt? We will throw this into the mix, so that evil comes to mean hurting oneself, harming oneself, being dissatisfied. And then mortals will no longer think about evil.

This is our card to play, but we are aware that some unfortunate surprises may be awaiting us; perhaps, as I was saying, that of seeing slip through our fingers the possibility of making them forget the good, because, despite everything, it will not fall into oblivion, nor will it capitulate. Evil is a kind of leech, feeding upon what is not its own, as it has no life of its own, and therefore it will inevitably come to an end. It very nearly scares the hell out of me to think that, if the good ends, evil will too. And so our malevolent mission would become senseless. Evil depends upon its rival, the good, and its sole basis for existing is the existence of the good, its adversary. But mum's the word! We will not whisper a syllable of this to mere mortals, and now let us not waste any more precious time. We shall start a new campaign of defamation of the good. And we can console ourselves knowing that, though the good may be unwilling to die, yet it will remain our worst enemy for all eternity.

Your very affectionate and devoted mentor,

Arcibaldo

III.
A fierce battle

Dear Polliodoro,

I have the feeling that I left you in a state of sombre pensiveness last time. We have received warning that we should be ready for some unpleasant surprises, and indeed, we must always be on the lookout in order to avoid having our weapon, evil, snatched from our hands as, in the end, it runs the risk of vanishing. Like a tumour, evil too can cause the death of man. But along with death, the tumour which afflicted him dies. Is evil the cause of his death, of his defeat? It would seem so. Though it is with a heavy heart, I must confess: the good does not cause death and therefore does not self-destruct. It grows, it suffers, it hopes, but it never dies. I shudder at the very thought of this and cannot help asking myself, "Might this not blow to smithereens our tortured craving for doing evil, for the pure pleasure of leading souls astray, that they might keep our profound Master company in his eternal solitude?"

But fear not. Neither this nor anything else shall wreck our plans. But it would be beneficial for you to shed some light on this inordinate urge of ours to do evil, this insatiable thirst for causing havoc. *"Unde malum?"* wondered Augustine of Hippo, that true bishop of olden times (alas, he found the answer to this agonising question) … Ah yes, I recall that you have a certain aversion to Latin (as do all those who are of a more pragmatic bent). "Where does evil come from? If God is good, why is there evil?" Such is the question Augustine pondered over. In order to find a satisfactory answer, we must go back in time — or rather, before time — when our profound Master, along with all our fathers in infidelity, stood face to face with their Maker. Let us travel in spirit to this initial moment prior to time, to witness a fierce battle. Let us contemplate with our mind's eye our fathers rising up against the Enemy. How they defy Him! With such haughty malevolence, worthy of our name, they boldly declare that they are no longer willing to obey Him!

I sense that at this point a question must surely be arising in your mind: "But how could they stand up in defiance of their Creator since they were created perfectly, intelligent and free, with no evil inclination? Perhaps their nature was already wounded by evil before evil had even entered creation?"

In this case, the angelic nature would have been created already tainted by and inclined to evil. But if evil were connatural to angels, this would demonstrate that it was created by the Enemy. If what you are thinking were true, the Creator would be the origin of evil.

This is not so, though many would say that it *is*. Stupefied by our way of unreasoning, they accuse their Maker of being the cause of evil; of being both good and bad; of being a split and dual divinity, with one benevolent and one malevolent face, one gracious and one grim, who does either good or evil depending on the time of day. This, in fact, is our technique to lay the blame on the Enemy for everything wrong with the world. Mortals have also become accustomed to this way of thinking. They blame Him for everything that goes wrong, and then they no longer believe in Him, they deny Him and become atheists. Sometimes it would give me pleasure to pursue this self-serving sort of atheism. Why shouldn't the Enemy cause evil as well as the good? If hypothetically He were the author of evil, it would still be possible for Him to be the maker of the good, don't you think? Evil does not exist without the good. And therefore it should be possible to say that the Enemy exists, even to an Albert Camus (1913–1960), who denied His existence on the basis of the existence of evil. It would also be possible to say that He is Goodness itself, even to a Hans Jonas (1903–1993), who held that, after the horrors of Auschwitz, it can no longer be said that omnipotence, omniscience and absolute goodness coexist together in the Enemy, but that He simply suffers with those who suffer evil, and thus not only tolerates but in a sense approves of it.

In reality, however, the Enemy's existence cannot be denied by reason of evil, because evil has no reason for being in and of itself but only in another; so say those who believe with fear and trembling. You must know, dear Polliodoro, that our fathers and masters of misfortune were not created with a nature already tainted by evil, but they chose to do evil for the sheer pleasure of it — through a desire to defy. Yet I somehow sense that, still following the same line of reasoning, you are asking yourself: "So how could they do evil if evil did not yet exist?" To this I would reply that what you think is true: evil did not yet exist, for evil only exists as the absence of that which should exist but does not. It was chosen, not as something equal and contrary to the good (as an *entity*), but simply as a free rejection of the good (as a prevarication from the good by reason of a freely willed decision). It was the will of our profound Master and of his followers to oppose God.

You may have heard of one of their more sapient sorcerers of the sacred, whom they nicknamed the "dumb ox", and who was so fat that a half-circle had to be cut out of the poor wooden dinner table to make room for his ponderous pot-belly (what a pain in the neck that fellow is)! He said that our Captain, his Infernal Lowness, did not sin in longing for something bad but in craving something good (final beatitude) in a way that did not accord to the predetermined divine order — thus resisting the Enemy's grace.

Evil has snuck in through what those of the opposing camp would call the wrong use or abuse — which we call the right use — of freedom against the Enemy. This is not a freedom in natural things, already perfectly oriented, along with our intelligence, to natural goodness, but a freedom to decide autonomously in supernatural things without the supernatural gift of grace.

Deciding what, desiring what? Desiring to be like the Enemy, while refusing His grace. Wanting to acquire through natural means what they could only enjoy through grace; that is, to be admitted to the contemplation of the supreme perfection of the Enemy and to His Presence in heaven. They refused the gift of being with Him, of being perfect with the One who is Perfection itself. They rejected Him. They wanted to be like Him but without Him, without His gift, without His divine life. "Autonomy" has been the predominant watchword ever since.

Because, at their creation, our ancestors rebelled against God, failing the test they had been put to, they were hurled down from the high heavens. We are rebels from the beginning. But allow me to elaborate a bit more on this topic, for your sake.

To our beloved fathers in infidelity, angels of dissent, a mystery was presented (another of those elusive black holes which defy our comprehension), the most original and unprecedented of them all: the Son of our Adversary was to become a man for the salvation of humanity. Thus He would have bestowed His grace on men and angels and elevated both natures to supernatural life. The angels would have benefitted immediately from this grace, through the vision of God. Instead, our patriarch of discord did not deign to submit to this plan of salvation. As was right and just, under no circumstances could he accept to submit to a God-Man, much less to recognise the superiority of that Mother of His, a woman of merely human rank elevated by grace to the divine rank, superior to that of the angels. How utterly inconceivable! That Woman, in particular, was the cause of discord and of a furious battle that broke out in heaven. We could not tolerate such humiliation, we had to mobilise against her, against her seed, and rage against her heel. Then all hell broke loose. We hurled ourselves against Him, our Maker. War erupted in the heavens. That Michael with his angels combated for his Man-God and for the Woman, and we, with our angels, armed with hatred and reproach, stood firm on the other side of the battlefield, ready to prove our point. There could be heard blasphemies, yelling, bitter wailing of anguished hearts, but also hymns of peace and adoration so unbearable to our ears. The battle raged on, growing fiercer by the minute. Many of ours fell. A sweet song grated on our ears without respite: "Salvation belongs to our God, who sits upon the throne, and to the Lamb." (Rev 7:10)

We know how the story ends. Michael was defeated and remained with those of the same ilk in the land of pipe dreams and high ideals, where everything is beautiful and good, where everything seems to follow a preordained plan which always ends happily ever after. We, on the other hand, by the sweat of our brows, made for ourselves a much-needed (albeit rather cramped and gloomy) abode, which became a place of trial where men are put to the test, as well as a platform where we can manifest ourselves to the world. And so the world, the grandest of theatres, with its great stage where the history of humanity is played out, belongs to us. All the world's a stage and this stage is all ours!

Whilst on the subject of profound biblical *rereadings* like this one, there's even a high-ranking prelate of the Church who recently learned the same trick — offering a historical-libertarian reinterpretation of the story of Sodom and Gomorrah.

The world (where neither orderly will nor freedom to choose the good reigns, but only freedom to seek the inebriating thrill of choice itself and the sweetness of self-sufficiency) was now all ours. We boldly dare to be free unto the end, unto the death of the soul, with courage and perseverance. They, on the other hand, meekly resign themselves to the freedom of an Other, and yet dare to call that a life worth living.

So we were ready to seduce mankind. From the very beginning, it was the voice of our Father which seductively made that sweet poison seep into the minds of the first parents. "Why trouble yourself about being obedient?" he said. "Why bother listening to the voice of your Master, who promises you a paradise, but only in the world to come? Listen instead to the voices of those who can make you happy here and now, promptly, without delay."

The progenitors took the bait. They dared to exercise their freedom, as our profound Master and his companions had originally done. Prompted by him, they ate the forbidden fruit. They disobeyed. The evil which then blossomed spread instantly all over the earth. The disobedience of the once-celestial spirits enveloped the earth as well. The deceit of the proud spirits also bewitched mortals. Thus evil entered the world; their evil, not ours, of course. Ours is the "good" that seeks to vanquish, though still struggling for a victory that has eluded us thus far. But if there is a virtue that distinguishes us, it is patience, so let us not allow ourselves to become discouraged.

Man dared to claim his freedom, to free himself from the oppressive rules of his Creator. Those of the opposing camp will tell us this is a sin, and that man, by sinning against his God, committed the gravest of evils. *Mysterium iniquitatis*: sin, the cause of all the evil in the world, entered the world and subjugated it. They will claim that moral evil — firstly the sin of angels, then that of the progenitors and of all mankind — is at the origin of every other evil, even physical ones, such as diseases, chastisements, pestilences; in a word, of everything that is wrong and makes men suffer. Unfortunately, this happens to be true. An initial disobedience, preceded by the angelic *do-it-yourself* solution, also caused the disruption of the physical and natural laws that govern existence. It is like a dam which, if dismantled or demolished, no longer holds back the water, causing a flood which ravages the surrounding area. Do you see then how our Father, in the depths of the underworld is not even the origin of evil (which we call good)? That singular and saintly bishop of Hippo intuited this truth — grasping that even if our profound Father were the cause of evil, one would still wonder where the devil himself came from. Alas, he who freed himself from the bonds of pleasure, and gave himself up to the Enemy with all his heart and soul, wrote about it in a memorable passage of his *Confessions*. Whoever made the devil would also have created evil. And so this brings us back to square one. We make the most of this sophistry to entangle the pious and trick men into laying the blame once again on our Enemy. It is He who must be recriminated for everything that goes awry, and thus we liberate man and ourselves from our own responsibility.

But if left like this, the difficulty has not been resolved, but simply brings us back to our fundamental problem. We can muddle men's minds, wrapping them up in false reasoning. The Enemy, however, cannot be fooled. He can do no wrong, He who is the Good — and the sole Good. Disorder, evil derives from an act of disobedience, in heaven and on earth, as I have already explained to you. This mystery prompts us to ask ourselves why our Wise Master preferred himself to the Enemy in the first place. Why did he prefer disobedience? When we have found an answer to this question, we will also have found the reason for evil, which we relish in any case.

Along with evil, in fact, was born the pleasure of doing evil. To do evil is to reject the good, but it was worth the pain. What we have won is our freedom, or better still, our inordinate desire to reaffirm it whenever it we fancy, without any scruple for the laws of the Creator. What we want is ourselves, our own good, our own happiness without any imposition or commandment weighing us down. We want to be forever free in our desires, without limits, without laws.

The will is the cause of our rebellion. The will is the driving force of a life truly worth living. We want no remedies to the absolute will, nor do we want limits. The Enemy is a barrier that we will tear down, or at least attempt to topple. Yet we cannot help recalling that if we did manage to do away with this ultimate limit, we would also be doing away with ourselves. So what can be done? We can teach men to transgress without restraint till the very end. After all, what truly characterises us is our envy of the One who is our limit but whom we can neither avoid nor eliminate. If He were not there, what good would our rebellion do us? We are rebels and will continue to be so for all eternity. This is a rebellion which suits us just fine, which perfectly satisfies us. Therefore we extend it to the world, but above all to the Church. Now, with my warmest regards, I will leave you to ponder over this grave matter.

Your fellow wayward wanderer and devoted mentor,

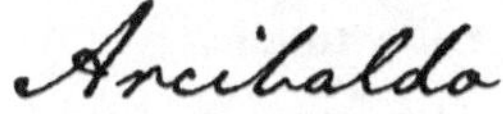

IV.
It exists but is nowhere to be seen

Dear Polliodoro,

I'm quite proud of you. My colleagues in charge of your group tell me that you refuse to entertain any troublesome thought that might disturb you or divert you from your duty of enlightening humanity and of indoctrinating those who call themselves believers. As you are well aware, our golden rule is to operate in silence, behind the scenes, without being seen. We prefer to go unnoticed. We convince mortals that everything depends on them, while in reality much depends on us. And if this deception doesn't work, then we make them believe that it's *all* our doing, that everything under heaven is the work of the spirits of chaos and incredulity that we are. What counts at the end of the day is that they simply forget the Enemy. In fact, if everything depends on us — the good along with the bad — then nothing depends either on them or on their Master any longer. This appears to me a splendid idea to get rid of that old-fashioned belief in the devil which keeps men on their guard. If we can induce many of them to be obsessed with seeing the devil here, there, and everywhere, there will certainly be at least one fine fellow who will react by saying, "To hell with the devil!" Perhaps more than one, perhaps even the majority? It is hard to say, for not everyone is so gullible. In any case, our Father of the sublimest depths will surely be grateful to us for any success we might have.

However, the problem with this dialectic of "yes, no, maybe so" regarding the devil is that, precisely in this scenario, that pesky notion of the "devil" persists. We must aim at gradually eliminating all trace of thought which might keep alive in people's minds the very notion of the devil, and then we will move on to the next step. The oblivion of any idea of our being the enemies of man should be accompanied by the forgetfulness of the infernal abode or the eternal condition of us so-called enemies, for in truth we are benefactors of humanity. In other words, we must also attempt to liberate believers from the idea of hell that they have drawn up for themselves from their Gospel accounts. However, for some time now, this idea has been growing ever weaker and increasingly inconsistent, without our having done a blessed thing — mainly thanks to the efforts of our allies and advocates who have managed to slip into their theological, or rather diabo-logical, ranks. From charlatans of the sacred, they have suddenly changed, thanks to us, to masters of empty chatter — and quite fond of listening to it.

We will certainly not begin by making them deny *ex abrupto* ("all of a sudden") the existence of hell; that would be much too conspicuous a manoeuvre. Rather, we could aim at inciting them to present it as a condition of such utter misery and despair that it would be unbearable to consign anyone to it, except for the devil (or for that idea of the devil that up till now they have conserved), along with a few of his subordinates. We will begin to preach our word, injecting the following vaguely Catholic-sounding homily, palatable even to pious ears, into their minds:

"My brothers and sisters in Christ, let us listen to the voice of the Spirit speaking today through mine, for I have something momentous to share with you. Life is an incomparable mystery destined never to come to an end. We live too often as if life here on earth were to continue endlessly. On the contrary, this life of ours is destined to endure, not in the here and now, but in the eternity of God. Take a moment to think about this destiny awaiting us. Let us ponder a moment the future in store for us. God has created us to be eternal with Him. This is our ultimate end and the cause of our joy. Sin leads us away from God and therefore we ought to avoid committing it. And yet, how could such a good God, who created us out of pure love and for our never-ending bliss, allow us to turn away from Him forever? Banish any such idea! An eternity without God! How utterly inconceivable and unconscionable! How could we imagine such a thing ever happening? God's mercy, which is as infinite as He is Himself, would never allow a creature of His, endowed with intelligence and freedom, enriched with the gift of grace, to be lost eternally, thus losing everything that he had freely received from his Lord. Let us trust in God's mercy. Let us abandon ourselves wholly to His infinite goodness, so that we can feel certain that hell will be barred — for you, for me, for everyone — by the love of a God who could never find perfect repose until each and every one of His children had come home to Him, and would remain restless, knowing no peace, if He had the slightest fear that even one child of His might never be coming home."

There you have it, Polliodoro, a model sermon that you should learn by heart and begin inculcating into the heads of your cassock-wearing patients. Insist on forgiving mercy. A mercy which liberates everyone from hell simply by moving it to a remote, inaccessible corner, or rather, which bars entry so that no one may enter. We might even let them believe in its existence, but merely as a sort of scarecrow. This way the dogma won't be denied, but it will be rendered harmless. Hell will continue to exist for the benefit of a handful of poor devils — for us — but no longer for mortal men. This will be the best way to precipitate them into the bottomless pit in droves, without much of an effort on our part. And if some of your patients are a bit fussy about what you serve up, having no taste for insipid blather, then we might try seasoning the speech with some more refined condiments.

We will begin by saying that their Jesus at the time of His death and burial, descended, with His soul, into *inferno* (no, your eyes have not deceived you: not into *inferi* — that is, to the limbo of the fathers, to free the righteous awaiting redemption), and by an act of pure mercy, liberated the damned souls. He was the only one to be damned because, in a vicarious way, He took upon Himself the damnation of others, of all the reprobate. He made Himself sin to the end, to the point of suffering the punishments of eternal condemnation for others. A vicarious satisfaction turned upside down. Their Jesus, therefore, with His descent into *inferno*, not only did not produce a negative effect on the hell of the damned, confounding them even more, but rather liberated them, just as He had done for the righteous. This is how mercy works. If God is good, why should He not also deliver the damned? If He did not free them, He would not really be omnipotent. If then He is omnipotent and He wants to free them but He does not, He would be lacking in goodness. What say you to this bit of diabo-logical reasoning? Not too bad, eh? Close your eyes for a moment, immerse yourself in mercy and — *wham, whoosh, kapow* — you're saved!

From here, then, the discourse can move slowly to the universal salvific will of God. How could we reconcile the fact that God wants all men to be saved (cf. 1 Tm 2:4) with the damnation of one single man? Wouldn't that be a contradiction in God's will? They might object that man, however, is free and that God does not force anyone to accept His salvation. And you will answer them like this (with homiletics):

"What man would freely refuse a love that has no end and instead procure for himself the evil of eternal damnation? Only a damned fool."

Then you will add:

"You men are no fools, so you will certainly not refuse this love. Be open to it and then don't worry if you close your hearts."

We will impose on them the love of choice without freedom. In this way we will negate love, but in a subtle way; that is, we will presuppose that their freedom is perfect and not tainted by the evil of sin (that too must disappear in the newspeak of ecclesiastical indoctrination). We will render them all immaculate and preordained to the good and thus we will rid ourselves once and for all of that Woman who claims to be unique and immaculate. Hell exists, though unseen, and woe betide if it did not, for otherwise how would we identify the gratuitous evil committed on earth? At worst it will be inhabited by the bad angels — and if you really must insist, by the most heinous criminals and cruellest tyrants in history, while conserving a freedom of opinion regarding this latter proposition. In spite of their Gospel, hell will no longer be a condition and an abode for "workers of iniquity", incapable of liberating themselves from the evil of sin that inhabits them because they are totally entangled in it. Like a truly artful magic trick (of which we are the experts), it will slowly but surely disappear, to reappear only from time to time, here and there, with some superficial fervour. But to which very few will henceforth be susceptible.

However, we must not neglect the worst of them. If your patients are really hardened saints stubborn in their righteousness, or arrogant traditionalists, there is another, newer doctrine which will do the trick. Pay close attention so as to follow me in more subtle reasoning, worthy of our profound Master, and we will have totally buried the idea of eternal damnation. Hell must not be negated, as we have already stated. Their Jesus speaks of it quite a few times. In fact, He refers to it more than eighteen times in the Gospels. Hell exists; our Enemy forbid we deny it. How could we deny it, who live there from dawn to dusk? But by insisting on the fact that it exists, we can also subvert its presence and transform it into its absence. We will say that hell must exist for the Cross and the Redemption to have meaning. Salvation without hell would be like being saved from death without there being any danger of dying in the first place. The danger is there, but it remains a mere risk, nothing more. A risk not worth taking.

The most tangible image we can offer of this narrow escape is the example of a friend of ours, Judas Iscariot. Judas betrayed Jesus, but in his betrayal there was rather the rejection of an erroneous idea of Jesus, of a distorted idea of God. Judas sold the God of law and rigorist legalism for thirty pieces of silver, as the true God was unknown before the Son revealed Him — because God is love and His love is revealed only and definitively on the Cross. Without the Cross of Jesus, Judas did not know what he was doing. Did Jesus not in fact forgive from the Cross those who knew not what they were doing? (cf. Lk 22:34) Judas — the symbol of each and every man, of the evil and selfishness that is in everyone — had stolen the mystery of divine sonship, the gifts of God. He thought he had pocketed God, as the worldly-wise Pharisaical Christians were wont to do, in order to know perfectly how divine things work. Judas is the sin of the world, the pride of man. But Jesus liberates him through His love for him, through His death on the Cross, so that Judas, like every other man, would finally experience a God who is love and not a legalistic imposition or a mere obedience to precepts. Judas' sign of salvation — be attentive, this is a masterstroke that I myself learned to my surprise from one of their sacred swindlers, who in reality is our sincere collaborator — was that "morsel" that Jesus dipped and gave him before he went out of the upper room to betray Him (cf. Jn 13:26). Since that morsel is presumed to be the Eucharist, the Bread that makes us aware of the mystery of God, then, with good reason, that Bread "instructed" (cf. Jn 6:45 with reference to Is 54:13) Judas in advance about the true identity of Jesus, the God of love, the Bread of life, the God who saves us through the death of the Son. So Judas was saved, no doubt about it. Hell is not for mortals, not even for that man of whom, until recently, it was thought it would have been better "had he never been born" (Mt 26:24). Hell exists, of course, but we have already put it to the test and overcome it. It is the absence of God who is love but who triumphs through the weakness of the Son. Judas represents each and every one of us. So now, we have love and no longer any hell. Abandoned and alone, it has been reduced to ashes.

A clever discourse, convoluted and profound, in support of a recent exegetical finding, namely that Judas was saved, and is therefore no longer the "son of perdition" (Jn 17:12) — a speech that, to our amazement, with slight variations, some senior officials of the Church have been giving for some time now (we have excellent allies within the Church hierarchy, intent on changing the content of the faith without anyone noticing it — an excellent stratagem worthy of his Sublime Profundity). In this way, it was possible to cloud that other passage of John's Gospel, when Judas took the morsel and left the upper room: "it was night" (Jn 13:30). It was the empire of our night that enveloped him and pushed him to hang himself, his heart being deprived of divine enlightenment. In the night, man gropes in the dark.

Judas is indeed a very interesting figure, to be studied with greater attention in order to convey our message all the better. But I wonder if it is worth presenting Judas with all these mental acrobatics. What I fear is that our excessive reliance on this figure may attract suspicion. After all, this idea of a Judas as a symbol of evil present in all men may come to be seen as simply a rehashing of the theses of the apocryphal (and Gnostic) gospel of Judas, dating back to the beginning of the fourth century and found in a Coptic manuscript in Egypt.

The main idea of that Gnostic text is that, if Jesus is the Saviour of humanity, it is thanks to the betrayal of Judas. If Jesus is who He is, He owes it to Judas. So who is more important, Jesus or Judas? Of course it is Judas, our ally in rendering the mystery of Jesus harmless and laughable. His love becomes yet another way to wipe out the evil in the world with a sponge. The betrayal of one of the twelve simply becomes the opportunity for Jesus to become Himself and to reveal Himself to the world as an ambulance driver who rescues men from the evils of the world. Jesus heals Judas, and so the idea that Judas wanted to overcome a God he had pocketed, to exchange his faith in the law and in a divine order for a faith in a God who heals all wounds and rights all wrongs, has returned with a vengeance and is now being imposed on believers. The beauty of this discourse is that, in this case, Jesus is not the Saviour, is not God, but merely becomes so, little by little, thanks to mortal men. He is only the rescuer from human miseries, someone they can cry out to when they are in need of help. And what then? Well, then, they can just as well do without Him.

So, my dear Polliodoro, I believe that by now, thanks to the help of our colleagues within their ranks, we have really dealt a heavy blow to Christianity and to their Jesus. In this way, evil is not redeemed, it remains as it is. Heaven, hell, and purgatory are all one and the same, and therefore they are no more. Now I leave you to reflect upon this, and I recommend you to be vigilant so that Judas does not play some nasty trick on us.

See you soon, your very affectionate mentor,

V.
Disarming notes

Dear Mentor, Your Immensity of the Depths, Arcibaldo,

For once it is I who, rather than being on the receiving end, am writing to you, because I have something which I urgently wish to communicate to you. I am well aware how unseemly it is for a subordinate to put on airs so as to be the centre of attention, to dare to speak with superiors on his own initiative, and even to boldly take up pen and paper and start writing without having received orders to do so. Though it is true that we have such rules, no one bothers to abide by them, so perhaps the time has come for me to break them as well. The situation I am going to apprise you of is very serious indeed and your response is urgently needed.

The other evening, while I was busy carrying out my first mission and studying in minute detail the movements of some of my patients, I came across something odd. I must confess to you how repugnant it is for me to have been assigned by you to the most obstinate ones, the traditionalist Pharisees who do not have the alluring smell of sheep about them, but rather the revolting stench of incense. And worse still, they always carry a bottle of holy water in their cassock pocket, making it difficult even to approach them. But you know how tenacious and intractable I am. I followed one of these unsavoury characters: an elderly priest looking as if he belonged to a bygone era, the sort which is utterly despised by the adepts of ecclesiastical modernity.

None of the usual ludicrous accoutrement were lacking: the slightly ripped cassock, the wide-brimmed hat, and the somewhat worn-out but well-polished black shoes. Thus fitted out, he walked with a slow and weary step around the neighbourhoods of an ancient city that had once upon a time been Christian.

"Well now," I thought to myself, "this is the real deal. A genuine priest if ever I saw one, who probably actually believes in all that rot."

We are used to being on the lookout for signs, as you well know. Under his arm, was a briefcase, tightly gripped with his other hand, as if it contained a treasure which needed guarding carefully. Some papers covered in ink, barely sticking out, caught my attention. I tried to read the tiny, cursive handwriting. But to no avail; what was showing was nearly indecipherable.

"Might he not be coming back from a meeting with other such priests dressed up just like him," I thought to myself, "and might those not be notes he has taken? Whatever could they have been saying to one another?" And so I decided to follow him back to his rectory. After a frugal dinner, he recited his evening prayers, read for a short while and went to bed. And so I had the opportunity to have a leisurely peek into those papers that he had been carrying. Now there they were in front of me, lying on a rough table that served as both desk and dinner table. I had all night to read them over carefully. And this is what I read:

"We will be 'hanging' until the end of the world, because man persists in his wicked ways."

What the hell did he mean by that? Perhaps he was returning from a course of spiritual exercises in which they had been warned about what is happening to the Church and to its theology in particular. On I read:

"Whoever follows You, Jesus, in truth, must embrace the Cross and participate in Your Passion and Death. What, Jesus, was Your greatest suffering during the Passion? To see Your Blood fall in vain on the soil of human indifference, and to see so many souls perish despite the gift of Your Blood. Your love does not impose itself, but simply offers itself, gives itself. If Judas had been saved — as many claim, even in the highest ranks of Church hierarchy — because your love would have freed him from a false idea of God, then you would be a god who imposes himself and who vanquishes because he is stronger. Your pain would be only apparent, Your love a divine dictatorship. We would have plunged head-first into pure Docetism. Thus You would be depriving us of our freedom. In truth, You suffered and groaned because Judas, and so many others along with him, would not be saved. Your Passion was real, You truly suffered and were not merely feigning, because You would not prevent some from suffering eternally. Those who with all their strength and overriding arrogance would reject the meekness of Your love, Your Cross. Yours is pain without measure. If everyone is saved and hell a mere symbol of perdition then why did You suffer? Why did You weep? Why did You shed every drop of Your precious Blood?"

Do you see my point, my revered Arcibaldo? This priest has conjured up the ghost of an old heresy, Docetism, which, thanks to our ancient ally, reduced the human nature of Jesus to mere appearance. Jesus would have merely feigned being a man, whilst, as God, He carried out actions attributable solely to His divinity. Therefore, the Redemption would be feigned as well, because the body of Jesus was nothing but a ghost. God took on the mere mask of the Man Jesus and played the most interesting comedy in the history of humanity. It is up to us, along with ill-willed mortals who join our ranks, to mask the face of God and give Him the identity of a god who is not present with them because He did not become man. God exists but He cannot be seen or attained. Consequently, man cannot become God by participation but remains in his sins. This is a convenient strategy, in order for us to make the theatre of the world the stage for our comedy; a comedy which no doubt works to our advantage, for not only does man wear a mask, but God too.

But if this priest, believing himself to be in the right, were to start spreading this alarmism, we would need to keep a cool head (I dare say we would not mind doing so, given that we are accustomed to a somewhat warmer climate than we should like). He might open someone else's eyes who, in turn, might start getting out of hand and try to unmask the true protagonist, our profound Father who would prefer to remain hidden. We are in a tight spot, my sublime master Arcibaldo. That black-robed, scruffy-bearded priest has caused a lot of ink to flow on this topic, and I have the impression that his reflections were jotted down all in one go, each sheet of paper a successive thunderbolt. He continues this way:

"Jesus, You suffered above all to see Your Church desolate, a widow dressed in mourning, where You have been chased away and where a man has taken your place, not in order to be Your vicar, but rather God as Yourself. You suffered because You foresaw the infidelity of Your ministers. You could already see, in the throes of Your unspeakable pain, that some would become like Judas, insensitive to Your grace, full of themselves and of themselves alone. They would administer the Blood of life in the falseness of their life and would be lost. They would prefer their own ego, material things, thirty silver coins, to You. And You shed blood and tears. You suffered for us, for Your Church pierced to the Heart, just as You were, upon the Cross. We are indifferent to this pain. Worse still, we dissolve it in a joyless and useless mercy, rendering Your suffering innocuous and vain. Souls cost blood, Yours and ours. But we priests have forgotten this.

The Church, Your beloved Bride, cost the Blood of Your Passion, the Love of Your Heart."

This priest is truly a nostalgic fellow, crying over spilt milk. He has not given himself over to the world, nor has he allowed himself to be convinced that ideas such as "paying with blood for the salvation of souls" are nowadays entirely out of fashion. Another elderly priest, crushed with fatigue by the burden he bore, spoke in just this way many years ago; he was an archenemy of ours, who lived in a small town in Puglia and who was pierced like his Jesus for fifty years. I dare not mention his name. But who gives a hoot about him now? Indeed, very few people, nostalgic for a time that no longer exists.

As I was nearing the conclusion of those notes, I saw the following and was disheartened:

"So, then, Jesus, has Your Blood been shed in vain if You do not succeed in snatching everyone from perdition? No, Your love is not superfluous, Your Blood is not wasted. Your love and Your Blood are the reason for our existence and, therefore, they will be the eternal limit and the eternal separation between good and evil, between the elect and the reprobate. Hell is as eternal as heaven. The barrier that separates them forever is the truth of Your love. From hell, this truth is perceived as an insurmountable dam, but rightful and just; hence as the perimeter of a love that has no limits, but which admits nothing impure within itself, nothing unjust. Your love triumphs in hell too, in that eternal separation of the damned — without imposing itself, without eliminating the truth. What we are, we will be. What we have decided to be now, tomorrow and until the end, with or without You, we will be in the hereafter."

This positively terrifies me! If such musings begin to circulate among mortals, surely many will be lost to us for good. We would no longer be able to peddle the idea of a divine and merciful love that turns a blind eye to evil, or even worse, claims to redeem it while leaving it mired in its injustice. Evil that is redeemed is indeed no longer evil; it ceases to be evil, it is purified; this, however, requires conversion, a change of life — against us and against all our seductions. Evil and the good cannot remain together because they are not mere appearances. This is because good and evil clash with one another. The line drawn by God's love is between hell and heaven. Naturally, hell is inhabited above all by those who thought that evil had been eliminated in the blink of an eye by God's mercy, without either penance, or sincere conversion.

Venerable master Arcibaldo, you must think of a plan to stop this haemorrhage of the indoctrination which, though it has at present a firm hold on minds, is nonetheless fragile. Souls are dear to us, and we want them to experience the warmth of our company for all eternity. However, if you will allow me, I wish to bring to your attention one last disarming thought which has arisen from the jottings of this priest and which inspires me with fear. There is a passage on the state of the Church that describes exactly what is happening today. This also reminds me of that dear collaborator of ours, that avid Protestant and a Communist priest-hater, who had set out to fight against what he understood to be the false Church, the Catholic Church, along with the pope, the main enemy of Christ. He was even convinced that he had to kill him, and had written on the dagger reserved for this feat, "Death to the Pope!" But then, he suddenly had a change of heart. He perverted to Catholicism following a vision he claimed to have received from our bitter Enemy and the Celestial Lady on 12 April 1947. This message joined the off-key chorus of another Marian apparition, that of Fatima in 1917, making the latter both more explicit and more comprehensible with regard to the events beginning in 1960, the year when we succeeded in convincing John XXIII to definitively lock up the message of Lucia of Fatima concerning the interpretation of the Third Secret. In that message of 1947, our former friend and now bitter enemy, that horrid Bruno Cornacchiola, possessed by the revelation of a Lady dressed in white and enveloped in a green cloak, the colour of hope, prophetically stated the following:

> "Satan has been unleashed, by divine decree, for a period of time: he will kindle the fire of protest among men, for the sanctification of the saints. Satan's wrath will no longer be enchained; the Spirit of God will withdraw from the earth, the Church will be left a widow,

covered in a funeral drape, and will be left at the mercy of the world. … The whole Church will undergo a tremendous trial, to cleanse the corrupt flesh that has infiltrated among the ministers, especially among the orders of poverty, a moral trial, a spiritual trial, for the duration indicated in the heavenly books. Priests and faithful will be placed at a dangerous turning point, and the world of the lost will launch a terrible assault, using all means possible: false ideologies and theologies! ... Then the Lamb will manifest His eternal victory, with the divine Powers He will destroy evil with goodness, flesh with spirit, hatred with love."

And then, even more shockingly, referring to a dream he had on 21 September 1988, the visionary Cornacchiola added:

"Would that what I dreamed had never come true, for it is too painful, and I hope that the Lord will not allow the pope to deny every truth of the faith and put himself in God's place! How much pain I felt that night, my legs were paralysed and I could no longer move, because of the pain I felt in seeing the Church reduced to a heap of ruins."

This seer has seen well — indeed, with great clarity. He knew a lot more than we do. It also appeared clear to me that the musings of that priest, among other things, referred to precisely this heavenly vision and message, with direct allusions, entirely appropriate to what they would call the present; alluding to what is happening under their benign and bewildered eyes, of which even that obscurantist priest is aware. How can we simply label him as being too clerical, or clericalist if you like, insinuating that he is completely in the wrong? And how can we convince our patients to accept a wrong interpretation of this vision, or of another vision that we might invent from scratch? Oh, how my knees are knocking in terror!

Your profound Lowness, a new, more up-to-date plan is urgently needed, with which we might continue to hide the reality of hell under the sumptuous drapery of some fashionable sophistry, and also make sure that the priests especially continue to read anything and everything under the sun, other than the signs of the times. I dare to take the liberty of offering you some advice: some pope from the 1960s spoke of new signs of the times, all springtime and roses, against the prophets of doom. Perhaps this is a course of action to take into consideration. Pardon, yet again, my boldness in writing thus to you, and accept my *warmest* wishes.

With devoted regards, your humble servant of the deep,

VI.
The method

Dear Polliodoro,

I understand your concern about what you have seen and read. But, honestly, what do you expect from an old-fashioned priest who still dresses like one? One who carries a bundle of papers under his arm, who has been audacious enough to scribble a few lines. Such priests are becoming ever rarer, and fewer still are those who read about the supernatural events you describe, and who know how to interpret them in the light of their Gospel and to relate them to their own times — times that unfold before their eyes like scenes from an old black and white film, perceived, yet unperceived, and less and less relevant to them; times that move quickly, but no longer have anything to say to them; signs that have been transformed into something else, thanks to their own way of deciphering them, no longer starting from the Gospel to arrive at the present, but rather starting from the present, only to remain anchored in the present, avoiding any thought of the Gospel. If they do happen to refer to the Gospel, however, they mostly define their allusions as subjective hermeneutics. Indeed, they are shooting themselves in the foot. They think they are being more modern by updating the Gospel, whereas they actually leave it immersed in its historical time period, without any rapport with today. They leave behind that Jesus of theirs as a personage of many centuries ago, who, if He came back today, certainly would no longer act in the same way as was depicted in the "historical" book of the Gospels — historical not because it is relevant to their faith but in the sense of historicism. And that is just the way we like it — like a dusty book on a shelf in an old library, which no one reads anymore, but which nonetheless enriches quite a fine collection of books.

Do not let yourself get worked up about all that nonsense. We need not worry too much about their sentiments, about what they might have to say; we can always convince them it is pure popular fabulation. What really matters is the robustness of their faith, an "adult faith" devoid of all this puerile prattle taken from children's stories, a faith devoid of the miraculous, of visions, of apparitions of that Lady of theirs, etc. What they really need is good solid food. We will tell them not to read such reflections, but only the books that matter. Books written by those who know how to rid them not only of childish devotionalism but also of dogmatic arrogance, scholastic manualism and deductivism. All that neo-scholastic stuff, which was far too stiff, rigid, and repetitive, focusing as it does on that friar they have dared dub *Doctor Communis*.

This is the method we must aim at. Indeed, what they really need is a new way of presenting the notion of faith itself, as well as the content of the faith, which, even if it has the appearance of teaching doctrine, is rather aimed at allowing subjective experience to penetrate into the understanding of doctrine. And so, with the ephemeral emotions of the moment, along with the changing of times and seasons, the faith will also change; not the dogmas themselves, but their way of understanding and interpreting them, their approach to them. This will then lead, though in a silent and discreet way, to exchanging the faith for the understanding of the faith by the subject (never mind if he be a believer, an unbeliever or an atheist — what counts is that he is a *subject*). Man brings the faith into existence, rather than the faith bringing Christian life into existence. Faith must depend on man, on his needs, and not man on the faith and its necessity. It will be man who will judge the faith and not faith the life of man. Well, do you not think this is a much more enlightening idea? But allow me to explain myself at greater length.

What we must aim for is a Church traversing a sea of confusion; a confusion, however, which does not appear as such but rather as the achievement of a higher stage, the stage of permanent hermeneutics, where everything is open to interpretation; that is, the stage of unlimited and endless interpretation, where the faith and its doctrine are subject to the opinion of a few, where essentially everything is relative. These few — their sorcerers of the sacred (or *ours*, if you prefer) — will be our closest allies.

We will let them sail into ever-muddier, never limpid, doctrinal waters; a sort of quicksand which is omnipresent, and into which they inevitably sink, but without sinking too much; a situation in which, for example, the pope is confused with the Church and the Church is confused with the pope. The pope overlaps with the Church and the Church is liquefied in the person of the one who, though he ought to be the Vicar of Christ, might also renounce being so for a variety of reasons. One reason possibly being humility, another poverty perhaps, and yet another a new image of service, which in fact enslaves. The whole world, and especially those people whose opinion actually matters, will give a resounding round of applause. But you are well aware, are you not, that this is our way of understanding all these virtues, as an alluring appearance that deceives? It is our way of officially implementing a revolutionary idea, which would not otherwise be accepted due to its explosive nature.

By the way, we do not *really* want to create a democratic Church with a collegiality that resembles the Strasbourg Parliament. Collegial democracy is a mere deception. It will soon be revealed as ineffectual. Yes, ineffectual, just like democracy in all its forms, which apparently appeals to people because it gives them the ability to take part in debates, to favour of this or that politician as their represen-tative. But the ones who really count are neither the people nor the bishops, they are rather those exercising the hidden power behind the people and the bishops; the power of the strongest who are, in fact, in charge; the power of those who have more money; the power which can be imposed through a programme, an idea, a person, the mass media. This power does not belong to the government of the people or of the bishops. Democracy is not the source of the truth as is often claimed, but rather must be founded on it.

No need for you to memorise this little sermon, dear Polliodoro. It is just to let you know that we are not going to focus too much on this form of collegial governance of the Church, because, up till now, it has borne nothing but bad fruit (and I think they have understood this quite well). We will try to turn it from a collegial democracy into a democratic collegiality, where everything appears to be collegial, synodal, democratic. But merely appears, and nothing more.

What we really want is a confused Church, in which the strongest (those who have more power, but whose victory is nonetheless modest, and who never brag about their triumph) come out on top. It is not the winning that matters to us, but rather leaving them at the mercy of a continuous, perennial challenge launched against themselves. In this way, our Father of the deep abodes can reign undisturbed. We will seek to breathe into dialoguing minds a model of the Church that opens itself up to the world, which dialogues with everyone across the board without fearing anything, but which also merges with the world. The turmoil, like a wind of freedom that we have blown into the minds of our worldly allies will then quickly begin to blow even in the minds of starched-collared ecclesiastical and curial experts. Let them feel the refreshing breeze of freedom, but in a well-dosed and prudent way ("shrewd" is the term that suits us best); a freedom that little by little becomes a spur towards rebellion.

Now, I'm sure you are wondering, what kind of rebellion? In fact there are several sorts, from the subtle, silent and pacifist rebellion to the extremist and destructive one, which ultimately all rebellions are. I am certainly not speaking of the public one against the Enemy and His commandments, but a soft rebellion, launched, as it were, by someone who, from the comfort of their own armchair, thinks of making something explosive, but with a long fuse: a stealthily moving, long-term rebellion. The rebellion that we want to inculcate in their minds will concern *a certain way of being Church*. We no longer want to openly contradict the Church. We have tried that in the past with the help of many of our model pupils, but it would be too easy for them nowadays, after all these years and in this technological age, to discover the conspiracy of the abyssal depths.

I came up with a novel stratagem. "Style is the man", as the saying goes. So, we will aim for the new-and-improved "Church-style"; that is, the *way* of being Church in this era of more enlightened understanding. With style, we will have free rein. We will call for a new style to replace the one which hindered freedom; which kept souls prisoners of themselves, of the norm, of the liturgical rubrics, and of authority. We will say that the Church is tired, she no longer keeps up with the fast pace of the new times, with the age of science and technology. Style is appealing because it does not suggest starting from scratch, but rather a rejuvenation, a renewal; giving yourself a new style, a new look! If you tell someone who is dull, boring, unremarkable, that they lack style, this is totally and decisively disqualifying, prompting them to change and frantically seek out some of this blessed style (clearly it is blessed). Try telling a woman that she lacks style. At first she will feel completely crushed, but you will set in motion all the strength she possesses to acquire some of that style she is lacking but thought she had. She will search far and wide, spend sleepless nights to remake her entire image — not just a new shade of nail polish or a more chic hairstyle, but much, much more. What she will be searching for is a new *modus vivendi*. A woman, like a man for that matter, will find no rest until she has found that blessed style. Who knows how long it will take her or when she will really be able to say she has actually acquired it? But she will do so at all costs.

Now, try saying that the Church lacks style. It will pierce the heart of many, prompting not just brushstrokes of colourful ink on the parchment of old, worn-out doctrine but the attempt to present that doctrine in a new way, with a new *modus vivendi, essendi et operandi*. A peaceful and sober revolution, carefully dosed.

I beg your pardon, I was forgetting that you are still lagging behind with this *latinorum* of the clerical caste. I was saying that this new style must be a new "way of living, being and behaving". Mind you, it definitely does change the way of *thinking* about the things of faith, because it is no longer the faith that matters, but only its *modus*: how it is perceived, how it is presented, how it is taught. Some enlightened expert from the United States has confirmed that the real question now is "*How* is the Church" and not "*What* is the Church". Just like that, with the snap of his fingers: not *what* but *how* the Church is! What a stroke of genius! Do you see just how alluring this "how" is? Who would refuse to embellish themselves, to freshen up, to open the windows early in the morning so as to breathe in pure and fresh air and get rid of that stale night? *Style* will do the trick, wouldn't you say? It is a neutral move because it gives the impression that nothing changes, while in fact everything changes, and keeps changing in the name of this new look; the faith will change in the name of freedom. And we might then add the denunciation of the "prophets of doom", as you shrewdly suggested in your letter, even if you were a bit out of line. We will make them rail against those "who always assume the worst, as if the end of the world were looming". Better still, we will even manage to make the doomsayers denounce themselves — but with *style* — averting the only really necessary warning: a denunciation of the errors that threaten their faith.

They should devote themselves to other matters: for example, to the world, to dialogue. They need to open themselves to theological freedom, to the inebriating thrill of novelty. And in this way the Church will become a laboratory of new ideas and enchanting novelties, open to a never-ending hermeneutic process. A continual draught of fresh air will blow through all the windows. The funny thing is that, once they have opened all the windows, they will not be able to close them again. Perhaps this is also part of the "open-minded style". It is like a hairstylist who opens a high-end salon, boasting all the latest fashionable hairstyles and beauty products, equipped with every novel luxury — even a tea service, so you can relax while you wait your turn — but which, due to a lack of customers, is forced to close its doors after only a few months. But no! the . hairstylist will not suffer the humiliation of closing after all her friends have paid her compliments and predicted such great success! She will leave it open a little while longer, then longer still, until she finally decides that her salon must remain open while being, in fact, closed.

Gradually this freedom or free-style — doing, redoing, and then overdoing — but with *style*, with *panache*, with true *savoir-faire* — can be transformed into complete chaos. We will not be able to say that we have won until they have even forgotten freedom. We *do* intend to win, but we want to see them renounce freedom gladly, willingly, out of modesty, out of humility. It will one day be possible to say, in the name of *our* freedom, that the Enemy, their God, is not so very important after all, and that there are plenty of things more important than Him; more urgent things that man alone can do, and can do only by himself, with his fellow men, and without God. No more faith, no more morality: these have only ever led to failed attempts to improve the world. Just look at the state the world has been left in since that day when their Jesus set foot in it. They tried to change the world, but without success.

Finally, our freedom will tell them, with *style*, to give up trying, to forget the Enemy and faith in Him. This is a succulent dish served on a silver platter with white gloves. Our gloves. I leave you now to meditate on this very base method of ours, dear Polliodoro, then to take immediate action, without hesitating. Congratulations on your noteworthy progress. See you soon.

Your master and proud mentor,

VII.
Major decisions

Dear Polliodoro,

At this point, the only thing that scandalises us is that nothing scandalises our patients any more. They see all colours and stripes in their Church, scandals of all kinds: (homo-)sexual, financial, clerical in general, doctrinal; sexual abuse of children and adults by priests, bishops and cardinals; networks of shady businessmen and schemers in the sacred precinct. Nearly every day, there is more shocking news. One day, there is a senior official found guilty of abuses against seminarians or young boys (very rarely girls); the very next day, another is found to be involved in some financial scandal in which the widow's mite was used for something sordid, but naturally in the name of the poor. There is something to suit all tastes, based on which you could write enough detective novels to fill a library.

Even one of our own who has infiltrated their ranks has collected numerous testimonies, all aimed at showing that the problem in the clergy is not homosexuality but the unwillingness to come out openly and honestly about it — the stubborn persistence in leading a double life. A point we will want to hammer into their heads is that doctrinal rigidity is a manifest sign of psychological imbalance, of human timidity, of a need for protection, which undoubtedly hides some skeletons in the closet. Moral rigidity (*moralism* or *moralising* if you prefer) is a sure symptom of some personal weakness that one wants to repress, or rather conceal, in order to remain anonymous transgressors in an institution that favours this sort of behaviour. Clericalism is a true disease, with everything covered in secrecy by those who know that ultimately they will not be held accountable for their actions, not even to our Enemy, their boss. If they continue to hide that a large percentage of the priests are homosexual, clericalism will only become more and more rampant and the abuses will increase exponentially. But ultimately this is only a ruse to divert the course of the investigation and convince them that clerical power is the cause of moral evil and not vice versa. They still haven't the foggiest idea that, in order for one to have the power to cover up one's moral misdeeds and always come out unscathed, it doesn't suffice to be a clericalist. The clerical abuse of power does not generate moral abuse; on the contrary, it is immorality, moral corruption, which generate the abuse of power. If a man were virtuous, not only would he not violate the Enemy's moral law, neither would he justify such violations and use his power to cover them up. If he justifies and conceals them, he is not virtuous. Clericalism is a very convenient means to let the real problem fester: homosexuality lived without any fear whatsoever, and with the intention of justifying it as such; no longer as a mere youthful vice, but a senile necessity. Anyway, as I was saying, they are accountable to no one but us.

And that is just the way we want it. At this point, they have come to the realisation that if the Enemy doesn't exist, they may do whatever suits their fancy. Let's encourage them to cry out for "responsibility", for "transparency", and to ask the victims for forgiveness for their dishonest profits and other wicked misdeeds. They know perfectly well that they have nothing whatsoever to lose. At this point, they have turned a blind eye — or perhaps two — to vice. Vice is virtue and virtue is vice. At this rate, nothing could be easier than to convince them that moral doctrine has nothing to do with it. It is rather the infrastructures that don't work. It's the controls that went down. The preventive measures put in place had not been fully verified and properly implemented.

Why do today what they can put off until tomorrow? They can shuffle their feet a bit before getting round to creating a new curial office (complete with a secretariat, headed notepaper and certified email) where everyone can report any molestation and abuse on the part of the clergy. They may be convinced that there will be more listening, more speedy decision-making — even when it is extremely painful — and that they will not have to keep forking out tons of money to the victims in legal settlements, without it being leaked to the newspapers — security protocols need to be updated. In short, we need to do more on the side of bureaucracy and otherwise leave things just as they are. The problem shall be clericalism and not immorality. There will be no accountability, nor any reference to our common Enemy. This much have we managed so far.

We thought that all this would throw them into such despair as to make them renounce believing in an organisation such as theirs, which, if it were only human — a sort of tourism office whose balance sheet has been in the red for years but remains open anyway — would have closed shop many years ago. Who knows what the people running this organisation are hiding? They certainly tried to cover up many misdeeds, with the best of intentions, transferring vicious clerics here and there rather than removing them and punishing them in an exemplary way. But I fancy that they are hiding much more than that. The statistics of one country, which takes stock of the situation in their Church regarding the sexual abuse of minors, demonstrate that the peak of the accusations was in the 1960s and 70s. It lowered in the 80s and then increased somewhat in the 90s of that same century; it then fell considerably at the beginning of the current century. How come? A great variety of interpretations have been given to account for these fluctuations. The dominant one of clericalism, on which I've briefed you, has now become obsolete. They don't believe in that any more.

They now tend to recognise as the principal cause the absence of an indispensable "human formation" of candidates for the priesthood. In the past, they had been eager to indoctrinate them, presenting in the minutest details the nature and the variety of the sins against the sixth commandment, but then this so-called "human formation" was neglected, to be reintroduced in the seminaries only later, in the years that witnessed a decline in accusations of sexual abuse. In the meantime, seminaries which were more angelic than terrestrial, with hardly anything properly human in the formation they dispensed, have caused these bitter fruits. This new formation in seminaries was more psychologised or more psychoanalytic. The focus of attention was now the human person with his fears and anxieties; his (obviously sexual) "taboos" needed to be re-branded, re-organised, and re-qualified. The concept of "abuse" was soon substituted for "weakness", "psychological immaturity" and no longer identified as "crime" and "sin". These latter words would have diminished the spontaneity, the courage to no longer be afraid of the intricacies of one's own subconscious; the courage to be unafraid of oneself and one's own body. Those pre-conciliar bigots had all been "body-phobic", and then, over time, they also became "homophobic" (a word we have suggested to them more recently). Thanks to us, they have come to see that the cause of the catastrophe was a rigid moral *style*, no longer adapted to a society in constant evolution. The body was hidden in the soul and the self was also imprisoned there. It became indispensable to set self free again.

For this, it was necessary to break free from an unjust situation brought about by the priests themselves: the power to hold man's conscience hostage, burdening it with scruples, useless obsessions and moralistic laws; a power that surpasses that of money, so prevalent in the past as to gain control of the world, but suddenly declared worn out and hurled into oblivion, along with what had been known as confession; from controlling souls to controlling bodies, then countries and finally the whole world. Is this not the masterplan of those great industries, purveyors of popular entertainment and consumer goods, who have been quite successful in overturning the action plan of some of our staunchest enemies — those they call "saints"? One of these, a certain Francis Xavier (whose arm was forever aching due to the many baptisms he administered) said, *Vince te ipsum* — "conquer yourself, and in this way you will achieve godliness and attain salvation" — because, as Alphonsus of Liguori said, "He who knows how to overcome himself will easily conquer all other difficulties."

And another irredeemable "saint", a certain Francis of Assisi, who has made a comeback by being elevated to ecological prominence, once said, "This is the greatest gift that one can receive from God, the overcoming of oneself, renouncing one's own will."

What fanatics! No, do not overcome yourself but be won over by others, by us! Fortunately, the efforts to put an end to the abuse that resulted from novel human formation have all been in vain. Indeed, as I was saying, it has grown exponentially. But lovers of (our) freedom have nevertheless persisted in rebelling against that moralistic style, which they say must be overcome, so as to be rid of doctrine and sin, in the name of a newfangled style. Just perfect, wouldn't you say?

And so, we will allow them to pursue their rebellion and to lay down their own law as to what is truly human and what is not. We who come from the regions of our fallen ancestors know quite well what is angelic. But we will let them decide for themselves when and to what extent a human formation is truly in step with modern psychology and its dictates, which vary from theory to theory, from author to author.

But before they regain the energy needed to shake off the millstone they have burdened themselves with, it would be a good idea for us to study our successes attentively, so as to plan better for the future. The information known to the deepest cabinet is not always communicated to all other offices, branches and ancillaries. Acting, operating, doing, as you know, is our favourite lexicon. But now, as I have been trying to make you understand for some time, it is more than mere action which we need to engage in. We need to aim at thought, at ideas. Ideas have a high productivity rate, and it is in the realm of ideas that we can come out victorious.

No doubt you already know that the dividing line between holiness and sin is very thin. Nevertheless, it is essential that you keep this firmly in mind. Every good priest is always in danger of becoming bad, very bad, just as every bad priest, if he converts, can become holy. *Corruptio optimi pessima*, say the clergy (not the fashionable clergymen, our faithful friends, but the old-fashioned ones); that is, "there is nothing worse than the corruption of the very best". Why not aim for the corruption of the best and let the worst take care of themselves? This, however, is a corruption that should not be perceived immediately, but should remain imperceptible; slowly and stealthily leading towards the ultimate downfall: the dissolution first of their ideas and then of their customs. Our trump card is always the theory of sin. It has worked once before and it will work once again.

Let me explain what I mean. The triggering factor for the profound moral confusion they have fallen into is quite simple. Like good pupils, they have entered our school which has formed generation after generation since Adam and Eve, our most exemplary pupils, in the first classroom of the Garden of Eden. There we convinced Eve and then Adam not to obey the Enemy but to despise Him in their hearts, to listen instead to the voice of our most profound Master.

"Everything is possible for you, everything is yours, but on one condition: you must ignore what you have been told — to eat from any tree except that of the knowledge of good and evil. You can choose freely, you can decide what you want as adults in the faith. The good is all yours and evil is only a means to achieve the good." Thus spoke the soft, persuasive voice of the Seducer of the abyss. If I may crudely invert their Scriptures, "Everything is yours, but you are no longer Christ's and Christ is no longer God's." (Cf. 1 Cor 3: 22–23)

This was simply another way of saying to them, "Everything is yours, but without God, therefore without even yourself. You will be thrown into the world without knowing which world, for what or until when."

The suave voice pressed on in a way that was appetising to the palate: "You will be divine. You will be the god of your life, of your choices, because you will be free to do good and evil. There will no longer be any difference between the two. Ultimately, in every good is hidden an evil and in every evil a good. What counts is freedom. Freedom alone and no more limits!"

Dear Polliodoro, this was an enticing invitation to spontaneity; to overcome the concept of moral law, established in the nature of man by his Creator, as the standard of every other law; in the final analysis, to overcome the limitations inherent to their status as creatures. Many of them have taken the bait, like an entire shoal of fish taken by a single sharp hook, though they are few compared to the multitude of fish and the vastness of the ocean. By overcoming any and all limits, we are leading them straight to nowhere; a nowhere, however, which is not spatial (indeed, once created, they are immortal and therefore cannot cease to exist *somewhere*) but rather theological. It is a nothingness of values, a spiritual void, a nothingness like nihilism in terms of its limitlessness. The ultimate realisation of this is our home, where those who took the bait of the limitless self — hook, line and sinker — will accompany us forever. Our home is the seat of the self without limits, except for those set by the self.

You have grasped, I daresay, that with the concept of absolute freedom (we might refer to it as "fundamental freedom" as it has a more agreeable ring to it) the concept of sin has fallen into oblivion. Sin is no longer a serious offence against the Enemy, a withdrawal into oneself and other creatures that one prefers to the Creator; it is one's own choice. We will make them boast of this "me, myself and I", chosen in place of God, to the bitter end; that nothingness in which we take so much pleasure, that endless fall into our arms, that annihilation of their freedom. With their prideful fall now unstoppable, might we be permitted to hope that their organisation, the Church, will also disappear? I cannot say for certain. I rather fear that this will not be the case, but we can ponder over that some other time. Now I have to leave you because I have other impending commitments. I'll be getting back to you soon.

Your very affectionate mentor and bearer of novelties,

VIII.
The big department store

Dear Polliodoro,

I must confess that I find myself fascinated by a concept that for some time now has been guiding the thoughts and actions of our adversaries, which is what they refer to as the *aggiornamento*: an intriguing word that somehow became the action plan of a general assembly that they convened for the restructuring of their big department store. What this *aggiornamento* actually meant was a mystery to everyone, perhaps even to the one who promoted it and who managed somehow to explain it, in a woolly kind of way, during the opening of an ecumenical assembly which they called the Council. There have been many such gatherings, but it is this latest general assembly that is known almost exclusively as *the* Council. Perhaps precisely because it was the first time they had felt the need to bring the Church "up to date" with the ever-changing times.

At first, many feared that *aggiornamento* might mean a more ironclad return to the law with an update of the Code of Canon Law, or with the convening of a Roman Synod with new rules to be respected. In reality, this word (heralding new meanings) was directly applied to the event itself, and even frightened those who wanted to open all the windows for a breath of fresh air, a refreshing breeze of novelty, a new Pentecost, or, as some dub it, the second Pentecost; a perfect way for us to maintain a state of constant ambiguity, which blurs the distinction between the public revelation, embracing the first Pentecost and constituting the Church, and the new, second Pentecost, being a new sort of revelation for a new Church; not a *different* Church, mind you, but a *new* one, if you catch my drift, a more up-to-date Church. And with lots of *style*. Thanks to this pretext of *aggiornamento*, in the long run we will succeed, slowly but surely, in making their organisation irrelevant to the world. Not a bad idea, eh?

There was a need to reset the apparatus. A makeover was urgently needed if their institution did not want to risk being left behind in the new cultural and global landscape. The old Church was left by the wayside. You understand me correctly: there was, for the Church, a "before" and there will be an "after". You must be fully aware that we intend to inculcate the majority of their sorcerers of the sacred, and not just our infiltrators, with the idea that what they call the Church is an extremely outward-oriented reality, reaching beyond itself, and not merely an inward-focused and jealous guardian of sacred tradition. If you wish, we can summarise this idea in two words, which one day will become quite the fashion: "outgoing Church", a Church that moves, that journeys, that goes outside to get some fresh air; the air you breathe in crowded streets swarming with people, like the Via del Corso in Rome or Oxford Street in London; streets brimming with the hustle and bustle of incessant shopping; where people live, where existence unfolds with its constant interplay of light and shadow, and its many unresolved *whys*. What could be worth preserving here? Mere relics of the past?

But back to us. I was describing to you the Church of yesteryear in order to reveal to you the Church of tomorrow, the one we want to give rise to in the not-too-distant future and which we could define straight away as "an indomitable adventurer in new, uncharted areas", in the words of the English abbot (and later bishop), Christopher Butler: an illustrious man of the Church (in my opinion, one of the greatest). With a rare touch of wisdom coupled with shrewdness, he continued:

> "The pre-conciliar Church was like a stratified rock before the eyes of the geologist, a fascinating object for the historian, not to mention the antiquarian. Curious clouds of glory lingered on from a past that was becoming more and more remote and irrelevant, like the three crowns of the papal tiara. Its law was articulated in principles, not to say in a spirit, which were ultimately those of Roman civil law. Its central administration was reminiscent of the family of Roman emperors, while its ceremonial reflected that of the Byzantine court. A critical eye was needed to discern, in the action and in

the theory of papal primacy, what came from the Gospel and what from Caesar. The Church had never recovered from the estrangement between Eastern and Western Catholicism, symbolised in the mutual excommunication of Rome and Constantinople."

And as if that wasn't enough:

"The *koinonia* of the ante-Nicene times had become the Latin *societas*, and that society, at first imperial, then became feudal in the Middle Ages. Again, in the mid-twentieth century, the Church seemed to be shaking and trembling once again from the shock of the Protestant reformation and, following its reaction against the new theology of the sixteenth century, it had also reacted against the whole general movement of progress in that region of the world where it still constituted a majority geographically, though no longer spiritually."

My dear Polliodoro, I could not have said it better myself. A true aversion to bygone times and to history permeates these thrilling words. History, for those who consider it to be "sacred", is not just a time that no longer exists, but the action of the Enemy in time, through His Church. Such a way of thinking was therefore an accusation against their God for having failed to make the Church a better reality. The same is true of society, which had been under the bad influence of the Church. It was like being ashamed of one's parents and one's origins. It focused only on the present, or rather on the future which was not yet there, but which would be born, or which had to be born, on the ruins of that anachronistic and unbearable past. But how could a new history be born if the one old one, which was such a leaden weight, were not left behind? It took a magical touch. That *laudator temporis acti* of which I spoke to you in a letter of mine some time ago, was suddenly transformed into a generic manifesto that read more or less like this: *ante huic temporis mala tempora currebant*; a desire to speak ill of the past took possession of many of them. Before this new and improved age, dreadful things had occurred, on which our musicians of the new era harped. The Church was sailing in stormy seas. However, it was not stated precisely when the new miraculous *kairos* — a true panacea for all ills — would begin. Did it coincide with the zenith of their Council or with the post-conciliar interpretation? Was it the "world of today", to which the fathers immediately and unanimously gave their benediction, or some time in the future, perhaps in a few hours, after you have finished reading this letter of mine? What mattered to us, more than anything else, was to accentuate dissatisfaction and prepare souls for the turning point.

In fact, they were in such a sorry state before that general assembly that their seminaries were overflowing and their parishes had not only a vicar but also a third assistant priest and sometimes even a deacon. But we wanted more of these deacons to swarm the sacristies and parade about in sixes and sevens around the altar, all of them together in one and the same celebration. We also wanted to see them married, so that they would know better how to dialogue with the world.

Not to mention convents and religious orders, which had yet to sell themselves to the first bidder offering a tantalising sum of money to restore their finances, shattered by the economic crisis, which had yet to become hostels for migrants and refugees, not because they were wicked and inward-focused, but simply because they had no room. These convents were already overcrowded with men or women who all dressed alike and made themselves known for what they were, without hiding behind the ecological (no longer military) green camouflage of the world. But we persuaded them not to be militant, to talk in a friendly way, as to a friend at a bar. They learned how to relax and unwind because the times were changing. Or perhaps the times were changing them.

And finally, we cannot forget to touch upon the topic of their participation at Mass. Practising bigots went there in droves. They could not understand a word of the *latinorum* of the priests, yet there they were. Although they had not been well informed about the value of discernment and the sophisticated concept of *actuosa participatio*, they sent their children to catechism and, stubborn as they were, even led them by the hand to Mass. They understood little or nothing, but perhaps they had grasped that this was the Mass and that there was no other — more entertaining and easy to understand.

"It's the Mass, period," parents said to their children, who would have preferred to stay snug in their beds or play with their toys. Sunday Mass attendance, alas, reached very high percentages, though, between whimpering one minute and making a racket the next, children often made quite a fuss. But this wasn't enough; renewal was needed. In order to attract more people to their Pharisaic congregations, they searched far and wide, sending almost everyone fleeing (and so be it). They said that because of the use of Latin during Mass and in the homily, the men sat at the back of the church to read the newspaper. With the reform of the Mass, however, they began going outside to smoke a cigarette before vanishing altogether.

Whose fault is it? They will say that it is ours, my dear Polliodoro, or the changing times, or TV with its enticing films and programmes, previously in black and white and now in colour, or YouTube and Instagram depriving the youth of sleep but entertaining them better than any homily could, since priests have no idea how to amuse people. Remember, my dear pupil, that all extremes, except extreme devotion to the Enemy, must be encouraged. We've been quite busy and our success came easily because extremes encourage one another.

The turning point had finally been reached. We must be thankful for that elderly Pontiff, elected because he was a transitional man — that is, because he was there for the shortest possible time — only until another, younger man could be found to take his place, for something more than transitioning. The real change originated in one of his memorable speeches, whose most noteworthy and explosive passage is worth rereading. Among the many things said by that elderly pope in his shrill voice, there is the following:

> "Indeed, the deposit of the Faith is one thing, that is, the truths that are contained in our venerable doctrine, another is the way in which they are proclaimed, but always in the same sense and with the same meaning. Great importance must be given to the method which, if necessary, must be applied with patience; that is, that form of presentation must be adopted which best corresponds to the magisterium, whose nature is predominantly pastoral."

He too aimed at the method! It's worth the effort of memorising this passage: "Indeed, the deposit of the Faith is one thing … another is the way in which it is proclaimed."

Doctrinal truths are one thing, while the method of proclaiming them is altogether something else. In more sophisticated language, borrowed from their charlatans of the sacred, one has to carefully distinguish the *kerygma* from the *didakè* — the proclamation of the faith from the doctrine of the faith. However, it will turn out that the content of the faith is made subject to its proclamation and not the proclamation of the faith to its content. The method of expressing the faith (therefore the way of believing) was applied with so much patience as to become the method of devising to no longer say all those troublesome things which have become so incomprehensible to today's man, even though they had always been taught in previous centuries. Method prevailed over content — the *fides qua* over the *fides quae*, the subjective over the objective — with all the best intentions, of course, to ensure that the content was better understood and better explained to the modern world, to the new world; but as you know, the road to our profound abode is paved with good intentions.

That speech, however, aimed even further. It aimed to adopt a form of teaching that best suited the magisterium, whose nature is predominantly pastoral. A pastoral nature! (You would do well, my dear Polliodoro, to memorise this, too). As if he wished to say (and indeed he did, for do not imagine for an instant that he would deny it) that the nature of the magisterium until then had not been pastoral, or that it had not been totally pastoral, or perhaps it had not been pastoral because the magisterium is one thing and pastoral care is another; the fact is that this magisterial address inaugurated a new form of teaching with a pastoral nature. That elderly Pontiff, in a new and incisive way, made a distinction between doctrine and magisterium, identifying the magisterial with the pastoral (that is, with the way or the method of proclaiming the faith) and not with the doctrine of the faith. There was a transformation of the teaching authority into the student body, consisting of experimentation, experience and time. And so there will be a prevalence of praxis over faith, of doing over being and praying. We will begin to believe in order to do, and no longer to pray and to be. Then to do is to believe. In that case, errors of faith may be allowed to swarm and to spread, because they themselves will find a way of amending and correcting themselves. After all, they are part of human experience, of man's life, of his being-in-the-world. The medicine of mercy will be more effective than the weapon of rigour, precision and condemnation.

There will still be a few hotheaded doctrinarians who will lament, because they will see the faith extinguished like a dimly burning wick, despite the more pastoral method. But they will always be very few in number compared to the up-to-date majority who keep pace with the new self-amending times.

"Not because there is any lack of false doctrines, opinions, dangers to guard against and to oppose," continued that elderly pope at the inauguration of the major renovation work, "but because all of them conflict so openly with the upright principles of honesty, and have produced such lethal fruits that today men seem spontaneously to have begun rejecting them…"

I confess, my dear Polliodoro, that I have never encountered a more pious optimism than this. This Council was precisely what was needed to give everyone a degree in social theology and the Church a conciliar identity. From this comes the dawning of the future. Everything will now have to be measured on the basis of this pastoral and methodological restructuring which will predominate over the mystery, the Church and the magisterium itself. And anyone who does not align himself with these changes will be an unwelcome guest. We will force them to content themselves with being unwanted guests in a Church that should, instead, be their mother. No concessions. You are either for the Council or against it.

There you have it! A before and an after, a yesterday and a today, clearly outlined for you, my dear pupil and diligent collaborator, Polliodoro. I send you my fondest wishes and recommend that you be vigilant so that all this does not remain a dead letter, but rather a spirit. The conciliar spirit.

Your very affectionate master and mentor,

IX.
Pandemics

Dear Polliodoro,

I would like to reflect upon our recent successful stratagem of spreading pandemonium via the recent pandemic. It is useful for us, with the benefit of hindsight, to take stock of our success, because it seems to me that, now more than ever, we must continue to ride the wave of division. Certain subjects are always useful to us because they divide public opinion. They are "divisive", as mortals have been wont to say for some time now. And as you know, "division" is so very dear to our hearts, as it is our Father of the depths who foments it. We revel and rejoice in division, but not because we want to rule like Philip of Macedon, who, in his determination to extend his empire to Asia, seems to have coined the motto *Divide et impera* — "Divide and conquer". Philip and his son Alexander the Great, though heroes and conquerors, are insignificant compared to us. We do not conquer territories but rather that which makes any territory truly hospitable: the souls that inhabit it — men.

Certain contentious issues in the public debate always generate a minority and a majority, which itself is broken up into alternative minorities. Other topics of political debate, however, transcend the merely political and are therefore all the more apt to divide public opinion and leave it divided, never to be reconciled.

One such topic is the virus which, before being introduced into bodies by means of contagion, was injected into the souls of many. We managed to foment division by persuading some of a Great Reset operation underway — a global reset, mainly economic though also ecological, and above all moral, aimed at facilitating the control of the masses, eliminating private property and making man a mere nobody in the hands of the system. And yet, we simultaneously convinced others that this is inconceivable, fake news, a mere conspiracy theory concocted by a few ill-inspired people who fill cyberspace with absurd videos. Then there was the physical virus, which at first seemed, by distancing people from one another, to be an obstacle to globalisation, but which then seemed to favour it by increasing cultural and social homogeneity, crushing everyone by means of a perpetual state of public emergency, forcing them to remain locked in groupthink, thereby preventing all veritable thought. There were a myriad of possibilities which we were (and still are) able to exploit, such as the preoccupying question of a military operation with biological weapons — more refined than nuclear weapons — designed to change global scenarios and weaken richer countries; or of a social engineering operation aimed at redesigning human society.

In any case, this pandemic was simply so catastrophic that it necessitated the closure of everything, with no concessions being made for anyone, arousing an ever-increasing fear of one another's company; a general "lockdown" (a neologism that would quickly enter all dictionaries and become the emblem of social standardisation): a forced closure of citizens' lives and, above all, of churches and places of worship. We wanted them to remain rigidly divided, so that they would not come to know the precise origin and cause of this virus, nor to realise the greater damage that was to arise not from the contagion itself — as our delightful virus would never reap as many victims as heart disease and strokes — but from the alarmism and terror that we managed to spread throughout the world. Technological man, constantly challenging reality, was suddenly transformed into fearful man.

Man kept in a constant state of fear is certainly easier to control. Alarm and terror are effective in eliminating any thought of the Enemy and of eternal life from the minds of humans. "On the contrary," you may say, "in such situations, mortals tend to seek recourse to religion and supernatural remedies more than ordinarily." But we have seen that the opposite is true. In this situation of general pandemic, men (especially Churchmen) were distracted by so many things that they forgot that they were made for eternity. This asymptomatic, spiritual pandemic wasn't the least of our weapons. When you strike at their health, frankly, they all go berserk.

"Health first and then the rest." Such was the slogan incessantly repeated by those mortals who care above all about their physical life and material wellbeing. In reality, this saying might have used by those who are primarily concerned with spiritual health: the directors of souls, priests and bishops who have at heart the greatest good of their faithful: their salvation.

For, in reality, *salus* — "health" — is a word from the theological and not medical lexicon, essentially designating eschatological salvation beyond this world in eternal life. It is not for nothing that those old-fashioned priests, who dressed in black with a bit of white peeking out at the neck, often used to speak of *salus animarum* — "the salvation of souls". But after a while, they set this concept aside, because they came to see it as bigoted, as incorrectly perceiving salvation as a private, intimate good of the soul, or even of several souls who get together and try to think about their *salus*. According to them, this individual (and individualistic) understanding of salvation had to be set aside in order to avoid transforming Christianity into a private and selfish affair. Otherwise, Karl Marx would have been right in declaring that the root of social and capitalist selfishness lies in religion.

They felt the need to aim for a more social interpretation of salvation; so social as to reduce everyone to what they can see and touch — their own bodies. Now priests no longer seek to save souls. They set out to save bodies. And so you see that "salvation" can very well become, with their help, a popular but intra-worldly theme, a horizontal vision of man, involving only himself and his fellow men. This supranational, global health emergency which we triggered was quite successful in focusing everything on the physical — not the spiritual — man, on his illness and recovery, exclusively on his body and not his soul.

So our motto, "Health first and then the rest", was soon to be on the lips of those grandparents who, free from the hassle of work, between a game of cards and a chat with friends, are quite preoccupied with their increasing (albeit not yet alarming) physical ailments. Active, young business-men in the prime of life became just as preoccupied with the state of their health. We even inspired this preoccupation in the minds of the priests involved in family pastoral care and of their superiors overseeing various support programmes.

The watchword was "vigilance". We played on their nerves. Life became a possible place of contagion, regard-less of whether there was an actual risk. We transformed all places of public gathering into hotbeds of contagion, especially churches — highly dangerous places where what they call the "Holy Sacrifice of the Mass" is offered. Under no circumstances were they to be allowed to remain open. They had to cease acting as field hospitals for moral plague victims. So we shut the churches, or better still, they did it themselves, in accordance with the motto, "Health first and then the rest".

"What could possibly be more important than health?" they would argue. If you don't have health, you can't live, you can't work, you can't earn money or even go to church. It is the most necessary thing. Without health, you cannot pray, you cannot fast; health is vital to everything! It's simply essential and that's that! So it must be put on a pedestal, and privileged above and beyond everything else.

On the other hand, nowadays men rarely if ever say that it is the devil who is pushing them to do what they would prefer to do (because it is more convenient, or lawful perhaps, though not always good). So let's make good use of this more-than-proven tactic of ours. This is precisely what we did in this case: we made merely useful things appear absolutely indispensable, whereas we made indispensable things appear useless, if not illicit. Health, we know, is useful, though not indispensable, nor superior to any moral good. (It cannot be placed before the need to observe the commandments of the Enemy, for example. Some fanatics even sacrifice health to do penance and save souls.) With us in the game, however, the useful became indispensable — and therefore licit. While the good, which is not always useful, but always indispensable, appeared useless and harmful — and therefore illicit.

Do you want me to give you a concrete example? Let's have a closer look at prayer and worship in the Church in this recent pandemic of ours. Is it really useful to pray in times of rampant contagion? "Of course it is," we informed them, "but not in a public place where the contagion was circulating." Prayer is useful, but bodily health is necessary. Therefore, all churches absolutely had to be closed and prayer had to be made silently in the secret of one's heart, without anyone seeing you and possibly infecting you. We even got their leaders to repeat it: those who had once fought for freedom of worship and for *libertas Ecclesiae* against the clutches of the ever-expanding political or civil power. Thus health was to prevail as an integral concept. And they were all quite content, obeying without batting an eyelid. Above all, we were gleeful that we managed to close churches, without their noticing that we were behind it, making a mockery of centuries past when, even at the height of the black plague, the churches remained open and sometimes even served as shelters for those most afflicted with the disease. A different meaning was given to the word *salus* in those days, which is why they used to celebrate the mysteries of salvation even when faced with infectious diseases, however harmful to public health.

But it wasn't enough to close the places of worship, which had become centres of rampant infection. We also had to foresee the eventual reopening, but with heavy restrictions in order to distance them from the sacred. We had to come up with something that would make them forget once and for all that sign of holy water which they call a sacramental. Naturally, we know that this horrid water makes even our Father flee. So how could we make it dry up?

In times of contagion, water (especially holy water) has come to be seen as one of the main vehicles for the disease. It could contain a quantity of germs deposited by an infected person, and others might become infected by crossing themselves with the same water. Hygiene comes first, for without hygiene, how can there be health?

This had to be clear to the new species of churchgoer, so instead of water, we provided lovely bottles of sanitising gel. Just press moderately to get the exact quantity to sanitise. And out with the water that sanctifies! The bottle was placed inside the empty holy water font, complete with a colourful sign explaining the reason for the substitution (just in case the faithful were in any doubt). Never were holy-water fonts so spotless as when they had become places of honour for sanitising bottles.

I don't think anyone was bothered too much by it; very few thought to ask their parish priest to give them back their holy water, or to come up with a way of distributing it in a complete conformity with the sanitary norms. (Why not something that sprays holy water like that sanitising gel?) No, they got on fine without it. Thanks be to our Father, they had already eliminated from the new liturgy that frightful *Asperges me*, once sung at the beginning of Sunday Mass, when the priest, solemnly dressed in a cope and equipped with an aspergillum, would roam the pews sprinkling all the faithful.

In bygone days, before starting Mass, the priest would be busy in the sacristy, exorcising the salt and water, saying prayers which were too verbose and ritualistic (moreover, not inclusive enough), and that perhaps he himself didn't fully understand: "O salt, creature of God, I exorcise you through the living God, the true God, the holy God …" And then on the water: "Creature of God, I exorcise you in the name of God the Father Almighty, of Jesus Christ his Son and Our Lord and by the power of the Holy Spirit." Then the salt was united with the water: *"Commixtio salis et aquae pariter fiat ..."* Mixed together, they were powerful "to put every power of the enemy to flight, to eradicate and root out the same enemy with his apostate angels". You *do* realise that they were saying all these things against us? Fools that they were! That too was once a sanitary and "anti-viral" way of protecting the faithful.

But back to our motto: "Health first and then the rest." The pandemic was sheer pandemonium, with everyone hollering, "Run for your life!" Everyone wanted to save himself from the virus. We certainly didn't tell them that neither could it be transmitted through contact with rough surfaces, such as church pews or other furnishings, nor with any solid substance, such as consecrated Bread taken directly in the mouth, nor could it survive in water for the whole time it remains in its consecrated font, especially due to the fact that our beloved virus is rapidly rendered inactive when the water is kept at room temperature. These were considerations which they simply couldn't wrap their heads around, as the need to ensure everyone's safety was their sole food for thought. Safety comes first, of course!

The virus was so aggressive that it even threatened their way of engaging in common prayer. We came up with a good idea to keep them from kneeling when they prayed. We suggested to them that benches and kneelers are contagious surfaces. Better to stand up. That's quite good enough. Indeed, standing up straight is the true sign of spiritual maturity and the surest sign that they have already risen like their Christ, that they have already been saved and entered into eternal bliss. It was no longer necessary to stoop down and kneel. We whispered into their affrighted ears that church pews could be used as seats but most certainly not as kneelers. Touching the benches by kneeling and perhaps leaving your handprints on them would become a main cause of the spread of the virus, so we had them seal the kneelers with red and white tape — the sort used to signal "work in progress" — thus making them unusable. This beautiful roadwork signage is a sign of the times: *our* work *still* in progress!

It is as if we were saying to them: "Ladies and gentlemen, we are working for you. Please take all necessary precautions before entering, or better still, be gracious enough to simply stay away, for safety's sake. Social distancing in force."

This was indeed the true sign of the times. A new way of praying in church: stiffly standing or comfortably sitting, just as certain ideologues of the liturgical reform wished. Previously it had merely been expedient (for some), but all of a sudden it became necessary and even imperative, just like getting them used to thinking about the faith in a different way, a modern way, more adapted to the present times. In fact, it is faith which has become superfluous, if not noxious, whereas the good of public health has become necessary, the only thing that counts.

And as for Holy Communion, which they henceforth had to receive rigidly in the hand and obviously without kneeling. With the usual excuse that touching the tongue or lips can be more contagious than touching the hands of the faithful, we accustomed them to think that Communion must always be received only in the hand; after all, it is just a piece of bread. In reality, they had already adopted that as a perfectly normal and commonplace practice.

With the pandemic, one thing had to be made crystal clear: the Church follows the measures taken against a disease and adapts to them, and it is not the disease that submits to the Church and its supernatural preventive medicine. The Church, imbued with divine wisdom, which always placed her at the forefront in giving solace and relieving souls in pain, would now be abolished by measures that would overcome the laws of the Church, that is, make the Church superfluous in the event of a plague.

This is checkmate, my dear Polliodoro. In the event of a public calamity and pandemic, when the Church has become superfluous and completely subject to civil power, even having to ask permission to do what it must do by its very nature, why should it be there in ordinary times of health and wellbeing? In this way, we have managed to render the Church irrelevant. We managed to separate them from their Jesus; to enforce social distancing between society and the Church, between men and the Holy Mass, between our patients and the Tabernacle. They were obliged to stay away to preserve not only the health of the body but also of the mind.

And when a few vaccines finally came out, we doubled down in befuddling their minds and divided them further.

The vaccine was to be their salvation, no matter how it would be confected, and the question (obviously secondary) of the moral liceity or otherwise of the cooperation of the faithful with the evil of vaccines, whose production involved the use of cell lines from aborted foetuses, would certainly not have to be posed. What mattered was that there was a vaccine and that it would be a panacea for all the evils afflicting society: the true saviour. Everyone would get the vaccine. Many, including leaders, would flaunt the moral strength of its soothing power, but no one would feel the need to ask if it was really necessary. It had become the new *salus*.

The pandemic succeeded in distracting them from eternal things. Once again, we served them a succulent meal on a silver platter with white gloves. Above all, we succeeded in inverting a famous saying from their Gospel, rewriting it in our own words: "Fear ye not those who kill the soul, but have no power to kill the body; rather fear ye the virus that has the power to destroy both soul and body in the Gehenna of this world." (cf. Mt 10:28)

The Gehenna of our world will be safer still. They have been seeking thorough and immediate answers to the present evil; no longer to that which is the root of all evil. They wonder why there was a virus, but they fail to see that there is a worse poison that we introduce into their hearts each time we incite them to hate, to disobey. From now on, everything will be licit as long as it is useful, but what is truly necessary, because it seems useless, will be illicit. We will render their Christ useless! We will render their sacraments useless! but always with sweet smiles and reassuring words, such as those written in large letters at the entrance of one church of the new pastoral approach: "Everything will be just fine, so don't worry!" They have no idea, in fact, whether everything will be fine, but they feel the need to write it — accompanied from time to time by some colourful design, such as a rainbow sign of peace. Why not?

Ponder well, my dear Polliodoro, over our recent triumphs, and please do remain vigilant because we experts in sweet venom, such as that inculcated into the mind and heart of their first parents, can soon find yet another propitious opportunity to move from ideas to action, from theory to practice. With my fondest greetings, I now leave you to your own reflections, relying on your vivid imagination. Here is plenty of food for thought.

Your very affectionate master of the depths,

X.
The evil and the day

Dear Polliodoro,

I have noted with some concern that your patients spend far too much time reading the Gospel. If they pursue this course, they will end up learning it by heart. And if they do, just try wrenching it from their memory! In days of old (long since buried), Christians would gather together every day as a family and read a page of the Gospel, or some other biblical passage, and the parents would explain it to the little ones. Nowadays, with good will, they read it on their mobile phones, scrolling thoughtlessly through each passage, but reading nonetheless. I fear that sooner or later they may very well come across this passage: "Sufficient for the day is the evil thereof" (Mt 6:34), meaning that man's life unfolds within the space of a day and, on that day, man can either be saved forever or perish forever.

Life is a day. Each day has a beginning and an end. In a single day, the whole life of mortals unfolds, like a painting is drafted in a sketch. There is no need for them to bother themselves about the day to come because they have no idea whether it will actually arrive. They must rather live day by day, taking each day as it comes and as if it were the last.

This day will never return. If it is lost, it is lost forever; if on the other hand it is won, it is won forever, because it is a fragment of eternity.

This is why the Enemy compares a thousand years of mortals to a single day, and why a single day is for Him like a thousand years (cf. 2 Pt 3:8). The day is, in a certain sense, the measure of eternity, not because you should live for the day, nor because the day is eternal, but because this is what it is destined to become. And unfortunately, it has already become so, through the Resurrection of their Christ, who entered with His Body into the day with no sunset; the day that will never wane, nor be followed by the night.

The day of mortals, in fact, is followed by night, a sign of our darkness overcoming the light, of the trial that is looming in the darkness of their footsteps and of their weary life. The night is also a prelude to death. They once advised those Pharisaic devotees not to expose themselves to the night, but to pray and then to sleep. Their Master, as I told you in one of my previous letters (cf. chapter IV), was also betrayed at night: the night of the heart, the night of the world.

Turning to the Enemy, at dusk and by the light of only a few candles that illuminated the growing darkness of their night, weary monks chanted in crystal-clear Gregorian:

> *Te lucis ante terminum,*
> *Procul recedant somnia,*
> *Et noctium phantasmata;*
> *Hostemque nostrum comprime,*
> *Ne polluantur corpora.*

Patchwork Latin, best rendered in everyday language that everyone can understand:

> *Turning to You (the Enemy!) before the close of day,*
> *From all ill dreams defend our eyes,*
> *From nightly fears and fantasies:*
> *Tread under foot our ghostly foe,*
> *That no pollution we may know.*

You do realise, of course, that it is we ourselves to whom they referred as their "foe"! Simply mind-boggling! But we'll get them back for that, and rid them once and for all of their desire to read the Gospel. How? With our Pindaric prowess. You are surely aware that the Greek lyric poet, Pindar, was our disciple in the art of rhetoric and style, as he revelled in making many digressions, always jumping from one topic to another without any logical link. What was most astonishing was the fact that they actually listened to him.

With Pindar's help, we will do our very best to say, for instance, that the most popular interpretation of "Sufficient for the day is the evil thereof" is not exactly correct. We will say it is not true that, in order to live well, man must think about the day he is presently living, without worrying about a future which does not exist yet, or a past that was but is no more. Rather, he must no longer think about this day whose sorrow is sufficient unto itself. We will graft the grief onto the day so that, to pious ears, the Gospel passage will take on a different meaning: "Every day is a day of sorrow", or, "sorrow is the sole day of man"!

The emphasis will be on grief and not on the day and thus they will become aware of a devastating problem, of an omnipresent theme: suffering. We will say that even their Jesus tells them to suffer always, every day, with no way out of it. Who wants a life consisting in nothing but suffering? The mere thought of enduring endless grief day after day, of every day being a day of grief, is utterly unbearable. This grief and this glorified suffering will get the better of them, and that will be that! We will incite them to rebel against their God because of the existence of suffering in the world, while He — perhaps unawares, fearful or helpless — does not intervene, remains mute and simply looks on (if, that is, He still has eyes capable of seeing).

He is a weak God who has opted for silence. He was accused of precisely this by a sagacious existentialist philosopher, Albert Camus, who saw in suffering, and above all in death, more than enough cause to be uninterested in God. If He existed and we were preoccupied with Him, we would either get distracted from our daily affairs, or we would give up fighting altogether. For example, a doctor who treats plague victims, "if he had believed in an almighty God, would have neglected to heal men, leaving the cure to Him". With God in the picture, what's the point? Men would give up fighting against an inexorable destiny, "since the order of the world is comprised of death".

These highly instructive lines are from a novel by our philosopher. It has as its protagonist a doctor who encounters a severe social scourge, the bubonic plague, which slowly spreads throughout the city of Oran on the Algerian coast. With the limited strength he has at his disposal, sleeping little amid the desperate cries of mothers who witness their children being struck by that terrible disease, he tries to fight and defeat what can only be seen as sheer senseless suffering. When asked if he believes in God, the doctor, manifesting great professional devotion in this fierce battle, replies:

> "... Since the order of the world is comprised of death, would it not be preferable for God if we refused to believe in Him and devoted every ounce of our strength to struggling against death, without raising our eyes to heaven, where He sits in silence?"

Have you got the gist, Polliodoro? "Wouldn't you be doing God a *favour* by ceasing to believe in Him, focusing on the things that really matter — science and life?" This is the question that we secret agents of the deepest spheres ask men of science from time to time, convincing some of them that believing in God is directly contrary to their state of life. Deep down, the doctor isn't interested in anything other than being a man, through and through. In fact, he says the following:

> "I feel more solidarity with the vanquished than with the saints. I have no inclination, I believe, for heroism and holiness. Being a man; that is what interests me."

They reject the Enemy in order to remain human and to be loyal to science. But they do not see that, in this way, the mystery of this life remains unresolved; suffering, even innocuous, can no longer be explained. Everything becomes even more incomprehensible, leaving them helpless in the hands of a blind fate. They do not see (by *grace*, we should say, even if that word is so hard for us to utter) that the mystery surpasses the science. Suffering, pain or even the plague join forces with us to rob their minds not only of the sense of the Gospel but of the very thought of God, and His being there for them as a provident Father.

As I have just told you, we do manage to convince some of them that science is opposed to faith, but not all of them unfortunately. There is a striking case of a man, Alexis Carrel (1873–1944), a French scientist and atheist born a few years earlier than our philosopher. He was a truly strange scientist, not because of his work, which was on suturing dissected blood vessels and cultivating living tissues outside their natural environment (which earned him a Nobel Prize), but because of his faith, which he was gifted with on a journey to Lourdes. *The Voyage to Lourdes* became the title of his ominous conversion story. In Lourdes, the eyes of his soul were opened and he was an eyewitness to a strange fact, as strange as his faith.

Being a doctor through and through, a scientist clinging only to his work, little did he think that the faith, in addition to healing souls, could also heal bodies. He therefore wanted to visit the grotto of Massabielle, not in order to venerate our august Enemy, but to console the sick with the only medicine capable of healing, meticulous diagnosis and therapy, to be renounced only if the disease refused to be cured and he found himself unable to do more. And so, to dispel the legend of miraculous healings — a response to an elusive evil and to the inevitability of death — he set off on a train carrying the sick to Lourdes.

But to our eternal regret, it so happened that he was an eyewitness to a miracle: an instantaneous healing of Maria Ferrand, a twenty-year-old woman suffering from stomach cancer — so visible that it raised the blanket which covered her on the stretcher. Her breathing was short and rapid. Another lady held a white umbrella over her cadaverous face, shooing away flies. A pitiful sight.

"Before entering the pool," says Carrel (who inverted the spelling of his real name to Lerrac), "the stretcher was placed on the ground for a moment. The sick woman seemed to have lost consciousness. Lerrac felt her pulse. Still disordered throbbing. Her face was ashen. The basilica clock chimed two in the afternoon. The wheelchairs, pushed by stretcher-bearers, arrived in crowds, among a swarm of pilgrims."

The woman was lowered into the water, with a good deal of care not to cause her further pain. As she emerged, Lerrac couldn't believe his eyes. He watched as, little by little, her face started coming back to life, and she began to regain her normal colour. The blanket, swollen around the area of her stomach, was beginning to sag considerably.

"A hallucination," Lerrac thought to himself, "an interesting psychological phenomenon that we should perhaps take note of." He took out his fountain pen and jotted down the exact time of the observation in his notebook: "14:40".

And woe to us spirits of incredulity, by the time the basilica clock had struck three o'clock, Maria Ferrand could be seen gazing, with an ecstatic look in her eyes, in the direction of the grotto. Her breathing had become normal, her heartbeat regular. Her condition was improving by the minute. The sick woman was handed a cup full of milk, which she drank in one breath, without giving the slightest sign of suffering. That was the sign he had been waiting for. Awestruck, Lerrac felt his strength failing him: the dying woman was healed. The most unexpected thing, the very thing which had been excluded *a priori*, as it lacked any scientific basis, had just happened before his very eyes: a miracle.

"Perhaps," Lerrac persisted, "it might be a *peritonitis nervosa*. And yet, the patient had presented symptoms that were too obvious and absolutely precise. Could it be merely an apparent healing? A stunning functional improvement?"

The doctor cut his speculations short and uncovered Maria Ferrand's belly. Her skin appeared white and smooth. Her stomach was small and flat: that of a healthy twenty-year-old. He placed his hands on the wall of her abdomen which was soft and malleable. The swelling and hard masses that had been there before had disappeared — and along with them, all the prejudices he had nurtured against the faith.

Alas my dear Polliodoro, stumbling upon a miraculous event changed his life. From a positivist scientist, he turned into a believing scientist, and so we completely lost sight of him. He even went so far as to write that "man needs God as he needs water and oxygen".

He remained deep in thought after this event, which had thrown him completely off-balance, and he sat motionless for a long while, holding his head in his hands, before finally penning this invocation (I dare not call it a prayer, otherwise we would be crying victory for him ourselves):

"Sweet Virgin, you who help the unhappy who humbly implore you, protect me. I believe in you. You saw fit to respond to my doubt with a manifest miracle. I don't know how to view it, I still doubt. But my deepest desire, the highest goal of all my aspirations, is to believe, to believe deeply, blindly even, no longer arguing, no longer criticising. Your name is sweeter than the morning sun. Take unto yourself this disquieted sinner with the tempest-tossed heart, the frowning forehead, who had consumed himself in the search for chimeras, mere delusions. Under the deep-seated and hard-headed misguidedness of my intellectual pride lies, sadly still suffocated, a dream, the most fascinating of all dreams, which is that of believing in you, of loving you, like those friars with candid souls."

That cantankerous scoundrel of a scientist, to top it off, ends up appealing to the Mother of our most bitter Enemy!

Who could have imagined such a thing? These men believe in themselves, and that should be quite enough for them. Remember, my dear Polliodoro, the grief and not the day, suffering and not life, illness with no way out. But enough of all this rot for the time being; I have had more than my fill of healings and miracles. And so, with my very warmest greetings, I highly recommend that you always be vigilant, without the least respite.

Your most affectionate mentor,

Arcibaldo

XI.
Just like joining a club

Dear venerable Arcibaldo,

My master of the rarest depths, I beg you to forgive my boldness in writing to you once again. However, I feel the need to apprise you of another odd occurrence. Indeed, I say "odd" because my mission of attentively observing the sayings and doings of our patients sometimes appears to be quite superfluous. It seems to me that, left to their own devices, which often involve a lot of studying and scheming (which they designate as *pastoral*), they manage to get themselves into the most exquisite mess without any prompting on my part. They go full speed ahead — but in reverse gear — with a watchful eye on the rearview mirror. The harder they press down on the accelerator, the faster and farther backwards they go. Do not mistake my meaning: they really want to go backwards! They give a fancy name to this sort of backwards initiative: *ressourcement*. The truth is to be found under the ruins of time and history, which are not exactly rubble but simply dust-covered bookshelves. Dig a bit today, a bit more tomorrow, and you will eventually uncover the purest sources of knowledge and the most authentic and genuine faith.

It is not easy to determine just how far down you need to dig or which stratum you need to uncover. As the new norm has it, it ought to be one of the deepest strata, the time of the fathers of the Church. And so, what about all that came afterwards? What of the organic development of the tenets of the faith from their fathers until today? Oh, well, that simply doesn't count; it's quite superfluous! They long for the novelties of the present age, or of this very day, and have cut out a big chunk of history to connect their today directly to the prescribed stratum. History belongs to them and they are the ones to decide when and how it is to begin. And what if that history happens to be the cradle of a mystery which becomes incarnate in time and speaks to yesterday and today? Well, once again, it simply doesn't matter. They go backwards to find the time that suits them. You will tell me (indeed, you *have* told me) that, in this way, they insert time into the mystery and make the mystery change with time, so that it is ever-changing, accommodating itself to historical eras and to those who know how to please their audience. This is what I have noticed and, to be honest with you, it truly startles me (albeit delightfully). So, at times my task seems quite superfluous. They dig their dead-end holes in which they no longer see the unity of their faith, and they just keep on digging for the hell of it.

It's quite a pleasant surprise for me to notice how division is fostered by the desire to adapt to the most convenient moment in history, even if it is one of the greatest — that of the fathers of the Church or at least the pre-Constantinian period. Not only do they split history; they also split themselves into different factions. We are divisive spirits *par excellence* but they, like us, relish being divided among themselves and never cease fostering such division. Entering their Church is just like joining a club — or two, or more. You have to say which clique you belong to: the liberal clique, the traditional clique, or some sort of moderately conservative clique which carefully avoids veering too far to the right. Among the latter, you will always find some who lean a bit more to the right and others to the left. Why is there no way to be a Catholic without labels? Just Catholic? They prefer to follow the course of politics, or rather, politics has taken possession of their faith.

It seems that these divisions derive from the party alignments that have always characterised a parliament. If you frequent a more accommodating school of theology, where the message of the Gospel is interpreted in a contemporaneous light, you can easily rediscover yourself as a believer in the club of progressives — those who want to embrace the world at any cost, even at the cost of denying their faith or selling it to the highest bidder. If, on the other hand, you attend a more intransigent school, founded exclusively on doctrine — no *ifs, ands* or *buts* — one of those that still teach that Jesus Christ, our common Enemy, is God and man, that He died on the Cross for their sins, but is without sin — then you are immediately enrolled in the club of rigid hardliners or traditionalists. If, on the other hand, you want to play both sides of the fence, and attend one of those schools which teaches the faith according to the latest Council, applies the correct hermeneutic of continuity and does not perceive any problem other than the hard-headedness of others in not wanting to see that continuity, then you have a good chance of being enrolled in the club of "moderate" Catholics.

There is plurality. You can choose which group to belong to, and deep down, this choice concerns personal tastes or subjective ways of seeing. Democracy welcomes everyone and tolerates everyone — provided, however, that democracy is tolerated.

"We are all in the same boat" they often comfort one another, referring to increasing social isolation within their Church. And yet, they are not in the same boat. They are in many boats, in fact, and we will sink them all, one by one! Everyone fabricates his own, claiming that his is that of Peter, or that Peter himself has his own, but not the one that belongs to everyone. Every man for himself. The whole is rejected in the name of the individual. Something is exquisitely awry, my dear Arcibaldo. How wonderfully wrong they are!

On closer inspection, the roots of the division are more remote. We must go back, at least to the moment of the birth of a more liberal Catholicism. Of course, there have always been divisions in their Church and, as a result, various doctrinal factions. At the time of St Jerome, schism divided the Church in three, and that gruff, spirited man himself wrote that, when someone tried to attract him to his party, he gave the following response: "He who is united to the Chair of Peter is one with me."

Disputes and enmity have almost always surrounded this Chair. Against our will, Jerome wanted to require allegiance to the unique Apostolic See and to the unique magisterium capable of settling disputes. But what if the magisterium itself were one day to become a cause of division and strife? Who would serve as a beacon in the stormy sea?

The seas were stormy when some Catholics tried to reconcile the faith with the ideas that led to the French Revolution; ideas of the unstoppable progress of human civilisation. Reason was elevated to the rank of sovereign goddess; an attempt was made to create a human fraternity in the name of man and his values; God was ousted, replaced by a mere Architect-Organiser of the universe, needed only to getting the ball rolling; social collectivism began to emerge from the Revolution, amalgamating everyone and reducing them to an indistinct mass in the hands of a few. Not bad, eh? Embracing these tantalising ideas, Catholics began to sow seeds of division among themselves. Soon there emerged the enlightened and the unenlightened; those who understood more and those less. Thus arose the difficulty of establishing who was truly Catholic and who was not, or rather, of determining whether or not one was truly Catholic oneself.

The goddess reason, our idol, had promised one thing above all to her worshipers: they would keep their freedom. They wanted to bring about the kingdom of freedom on earth. You rightly taught me, dear Arcibaldo, that we are the heralds of this reign and always will be. Freedom not to serve but to enslave and exploit. This was our manifesto and will also be theirs.

Then there was a priest, unfaithful to his vocation and to the doctrine of the faith in order to remain faithful to freedom of conscience and of the press — who summarised his dissent towards religion in a famous phrase: "All friends of religion must understand that it is in need of only one thing: freedom."

He desired unlimited freedom; above all, a freedom from the Church and the pope. He was called Félicité de Lamennais (1782–1854). He went to such great lengths to bring grist to our mill, and give us aid and succour. For him, the religious cause of the pope was identified with the social cause of the people. Defending the pope and being on the side of the Petrine Chair meant taking the interests of the people, mistreated by the aristocratic class, to heart. It was necessary to give a voice back to the people by restoring freedom of conscience, understood to entail the primacy of the subject over the truth and the faith. Free conscience was to have its highest expression in the freedom of the press, which implied the strict separation of Church and State, of faith and politics. It was also expressed in Lamennais abandoning his Church and his clerical state in order to devote himself to being a politician. From a monarchist, he became a republican, but not without first experimenting with other ideas.

Fr Philippe Gerbet (1798–1864), who was born in the midst of the revolutionary rumblings, was a bitter enemy of his, though not without Christian charity, and he wept for Lamennais's defection. In 1841, Gerbet published a book on the new doctrines of Lamennais, calling him a "Jewish renegade of political parties", since "he was successively a monarchist like Bonald and the chamber of 1815, a Bourbon like Chateaubriand, an ultra-royalist like the White Flag legitimists, seditious like the Duke of Guise and democratic like Carrel". A little bit of everything.

Gerbet adds that Lamennais offered "prayers in which he no longer believed, and the sole reason why I take up arms against the friend of my youth is to fight the enemy of all that I love with an eternal love."

Who did this poor Gerbet love? The pope, whom he defined as the "venerable old man whom all of Christendom hails with the name of father", whom his enemy had ridiculed.

Lamennais, according to Gerbet, had allowed himself to be seduced by the greatest Protestant heresy, which he summed up as "considering all Christian dogmas to be indifferent, and reducing the essence of Christianity to the unique precept of human fraternity. The new heresy, as we will see, irresistibly leads to conceiving Christianity in this way."

Then with an angry look at his friend, whom he abhorred for his heresy but continued to pray for, he added:

"And in truth, you preach in the name of Christian charity an equality and a freedom incompatible with the foun-
dations of the social order, and you are on the brink of
transforming the Cross of Christ into an arsonist's torch,
which you use to set fire to this social order, and you are
on the verge of digging the crater of a volcano upon
Calvary itself. The new heresy works towards this goal."

The Protestant heresy found its continuation in the revolutionary fallacy and in many men of good will who, like
Lamennais, tried to surpass it by embracing its underlying
ideas. The real name of this heresy was deism: a revolution
against God.

"God exists but does not speak, and if he speaks we will
not listen to him." This was the quintessence of Lammenais's
teaching. The revolution will press on in the name of freedom from God and its peak will be reached with the resolute
determination to overturn the natural order by leveraging
the field of praxis. Gradually, it is praxis that will establish
itself as the tribunal where history and individuals, ideas
and men, will be judged and possibly sentenced according
to their productivity and power to bring about change — to
subvert order. The task of philosophers will no longer be to
understand the world, but to transform it.

The most productive idea of this transformation will
be Marxism and its most successful policy Communism,
as a dialectic between the denial of reality and its positive
overcoming by means of praxis. I recall that the Mother

of our bitter Enemy appeared in Fatima in 1917, as you reminded me in one of our off-record conversations, and warned the world that Communism would acquire a cultural hegemony which would then spread from the USSR throughout the world and even the Church. The remedy (happily ignored) was the Consecration of Russia to her Immaculate Heart. By reason of dialogue and prudence, we convinced their pope to refrain from mentioning Russia in their prayers: it would have been anachronistic and, moreover, perilous. Oddly enough, this was finally done by one you would have least expected! What a nasty turn of events that was!

The foul waters of the dark wave of Communism thus hit the coasts of every nation and eroded its resilience — even the rock of Peter, which was the only one which might really have been able to resist. Fortunately, there were mature "adult Catholics", especially those who espoused those old theses of Modernism, a marvellous mishmash of ideas, gathering together the very best of Protestantism, which are so dear to us. They followed the path of "historical compromise", presenting the Enemy as the very embodiment of pressing social issues: our partner and even our brother.

A political outlook got the upper hand and took precedence over the faith and the way of teaching it. There were calls for a just autonomy of temporal realities. But it was more a matter of political autonomy. In fact, it meant nothing other than a separation of man from his Creator. So there were the dissenting Catholics and those who, with an even more mature faith, approved of divorce and then abortion, and then everything else under the sun which they might approve of. In good conscience, they could not impose their "Christian vision" on others. The natural law, and perhaps faith too, had become a subjective question, hidden in the profound secret of personal conscience, without anyone being able to catch a glimpse of it. Yes, conscience will be the tribunal of human history (and of Catholics in particular), where political ideas will be acquitted or condemned. Yet I ask myself, out of curiosity, my dear mentor Arcibaldo, can there be a division within the conscience of one and the same man, between his political conscience and his supernatural faith? How many men are there in the man who lives and who believes?

But once it has reached its apogee, praxis will pursue the same historical path as Communism, which finally imploded, testifying to the failure of this utopian project to crush people in one mass in the name of a materialist religion. Perhaps it was not enough to cover over everything with the excuse of the socio-economic alienation of man. The Revolution — every revolution — inexorably brings about its own destruction and reveals its true face in an underlying nihilism, in a continuous falling into uncertainty and chaos. But chaos is precisely what counts for us. In chaos, the strongest reign supreme.

Communism will fall but not Marxism; the political vision will decline but not the philosophy of praxis, which will be firmly embedded in the very marrow of society and of the

Church, leading even to the justification of a freedom to choose against what is established by nature — that likeness of a nasty old mother-in-law.

Our freedom both frees and divides them. It all started with the utopian idea that the only legitimate state is that in which everyone is either equally instructed or equally ignorant. All or none! If everyone is educated, you can bid farewell to the cultivation of the land, to arts and crafts and to freshly baked bread. This equality could only ever be achieved at the cost of the abolition of man. But if all are ignorant, this would be labelled as injustice by the liberals.

If a portion of mankind were to cultivate its spiritual life, said that strange Fr Gerbet, it would be accused of being a usurper, of being intent on lording it over the others. Thus, society being laid on a Procrustean bed, there would be a chopping off not of the feet but the head of humanity. These were the consequences with which humanity would be confronted thanks to the revolutionary process that would be triggered and which would now be inexorable, given the premises.

How will the Church respond to this? There will be those who oppose the decline, wishing to return to an irreplaceable medieval and Christian social model in the name of an ultramontanist vision, and there will be those who wish to go all the way, invoking the inexorability of the principle of modernity — that is, the primacy of the subject and of conscience over being and reality. The primacy of the self will be the primacy of the will: of the absolute will, detached from truth, goodness and beauty.

This division has continued up to the present day and still separates them. There are friends of the return to the only truthful social model — that of the *societas christiana* — and friends of the autonomy of the social and political sphere with respect to faith and theology, privileging the entry of the *res publica* into the faith and ensuring that faith be conformed to politics, understood as the planning of history and society, instead of conforming politics to faith. I do not deny that there is also a more centrist vision, hoping for the wise use of the principles of modernity. To a large extent, however, metaphysical philosophy has been replaced by sociology; and theology by (practical, not theoretical) politics.

It could happen that a certain ultramontanist vision, always privileging the position of the pope, not only in matters of faith, but above all in political choices, will one day become, perhaps unconsciously, the pathway to a papolatry in which the pope will place himself above the Church and even against it. In the name of the pope, doctrine and the faith might themselves be made subject to praxis and judged by the tribunal of the subjective — or collective (it does not make much of a difference) — conscience of the majority. The ultramontanists will accuse the liberals of favouring this deviation, whilst the liberals will accuse the ultramontanists of obstructing it unjustly.

Dear Arcibaldo, it seems to me, after all, that the source of the problem can be found in a forgetfulness of the concept of "hierarchy": they do not want there to be someone at the top and someone at the bottom, but everyone to be at the bottom. And we second that motion, for it doesn't prevent someone from imposing himself by force, as a kind of watchful eye on behalf of the collective conscience. It all favours the confusion that suits our fancy and fosters their division. Many of them believe that faith no longer has the power to change man's fate; it is rather man's fate which has begun to teach them how to live the faith in this world.

A spirit of heresy had crept in amongst them, expelling original sin from history and pitching in its place the tent of dialogue with everyone, even with our most profound Father who managed to get their progenitors to dialogue on a subject that admitted neither discussion about the right hermeneutic approach, nor difference of opinion. But the expelling of sin from history began the dialectical process of its self-redemption without the Enemy's help, with the full assent of our pious and devoted patients.

Obviously, I will do my very best to hide that famous saying, *In necessariis unitas, in dubiis libertas, in omnibus caritas* — "Unity in necessary things (of faith and doctrine), freedom in uncertain things, and charity in all things". It seems that there is no charity amongst them. And how could there be, if doubtful and disputable things concerning faith and morals are deemed necessary?

Voilà. I wanted to point out this wound in them. It will help in bringing to fruition the subversive process that we began a long time ago, when, with great pride, we breathed into the minds of our proto-patients the desire to act with full freedom, as if God did not exist. It is now sufficient to apply the slightest pressure on the minds and hearts of our patients to make them follow suit. In reality, they would all have done the same. But this is the subject of another discussion, which I am not going to embark upon just now lest I seem overeager. Please pardon my boldness and accept the expression of my deep respect. Finally, I would like to reiterate my willingness to establish the kingdom of freedom on earth.

Your most affectionate disciple and traveling companion,

Palliodoro

XII.
The truth

Dear Polliodoro,

It was with some surprise mingled with consternation that I remarked the audacity with which you dared intervene in this complex matter of the division amongst our special patients. But to my satisfaction, I also noted that, for a pragmatic spirit, you have become surprisingly thoughtful and theoretical; not bad for a novice tempter. As you expertly pointed out, for some time now, they have not required much attention from us. They are divided amongst themselves and are struggling to find the path to reconcile these divisions. Who knows if there will be any such reconciliation when their Lord returns? Perhaps there won't be the least remnant of that faith which is necessary to appear in His presence.

I do not condemn your boldness, but I do wish to impress upon you the need to be more prudent. The question of dissension between Christians cannot be resolved as if it were a mere political matter or a simple belonging to a club. We, as you well know, remain the main protagonists of this antagonism (which we can call fraternal but which remains no less antagonistic): keeping them at war with one another, so that they remain divided. Remember that it is they who are divided. We cannot be.

As their Master said, perfectly identifying the *punctum dolens* (with all your assiduous studies, all this *latinorum* should be a piece of cake by now), "And if Satan also be divided against himself, how shall his kingdom stand?" (Lk 11:18)

Since we are not divided against one another, I cannot lie to you; I have to tell you the truth, pure and simple. Our mission is to lie to others, to deceive them, to lead them down the path of perdition. For your patients, the truth will be packaged as a falsehood, and vice versa. We make truths seem mendacious and lies verisimilitudinous. We profound masters from the lower regions know how to spin a falsehood so convincingly as to make it look like the Gospel truth. Listen very carefully to what I'm going to say now.

Their division does not reside in diverging approaches to modernity, or to the principles of the French Revolution, which was its most perfect expression and would definitively split them into factions — the ultramontanists always siding with the Chair of Peter, and the liberals forever invoking the separation of throne and altar, of Church and state, to guarantee everyone the political freedom which is so essential for being fully human. It is not modernity that is definitive and irreversible, but tradition. Modernity, or rather the modern age, is a historical process and, like any other historical process, is contingent. Tradition is not contingent. It comes from above, preceding history and surpassing it in a timeless dimension. It is the transmitting of the truth of their Christ and their Church to every place and time.

The truth alone will never pass away. Tradition ends where the truth is bequeathed once and for all. Tradition will one day come to an end; the truth will not. But it seems to me that this has become a matter of indifference to them. They have completely lost sight of the truth thanks to our tireless work of persuasion and propaganda. They fear the truth. It is deemed intolerant, more divisive than we are ourselves. But the truth is to be found neither on the right nor on the left but where the Enemy is. The truth is necessarily meta-historical and can only be eternal. It descends into time to lead men to eternity. My dear Polliodoro, the truth must be carefully hidden from their sight with the help of such cleverly formulated sophisms that they consign it to the past forever. All this is essential to our mission. Only in this way will we be sure of winning the battle for souls.

However, this also prompts me to bring to your attention a strange situation. As I was saying, I cannot lie to you. The other day I too was returning from an evening patrol. Having ventured into the woods — not to hunt prey but only to scout out the territory and find out if there was anything worth hunting — I came across a man. His physical appearance spoke volumes. He was a middle-aged man with a thick and well-groomed beard, his light brown eyes wide open as if in deep wonder. He looked like a man lost in his own thoughts, one of those chaps who do not content themselves with thinking from time to time, but who make it the heart and soul of their existence. He appeared to be sad, reading a half-yellowed and crumpled journal with a melancholic but ironic air. Intrigued as I was, I approached and peeked round in order to read along with him. I had never done such a thing before and reading sideways made me nauseous. More sickening, however, was the text by an author from the not too distant past, the sort of "witness to the truth" that we devils would much prefer no longer existed, or better still, had never existed in the first place. Self-important conformists! It seems they are not made for this world. He was one of those who even now go about shamelessly speaking of truth, and who see in the truth the way out of every historical *impasse* to which we lead them. How dreadful for them! They prefer to isolate themselves, instead of shouting angrily along with the masses about how it is pure fundamentalism to affirm the existence of truth and to deny its relativity.

That text, a cross between poetry and prose, which I wish I could forget along with that man's face, was a sort of contemporary hymn to truth. And since I told you that I cannot hide the truth from you, I feel I ought to acquaint you with what I read, though it still leaves me feeling perplexed.

"The truth, like a beautiful but formidable lady, frightens us. She tells us we need to change. At times she humiliates us, at others she puzzles us. We seek to rid ourselves of her immediately by saying that she doesn't matter, drowning out her voice in a sea of the most disparate and subjective thoughts. We attempt to silence her, to muzzle her, to prevent ourselves from welcoming her by making sure we all turn our backs. Even so, she will not give up. She always makes a comeback, freeing herself from the stranglehold of lies. There she stands on the threshold of our heart's home and awaits our return. She remains there faithfully and patiently, knowing that sooner or later we must eventually come back home. A prodigal son cannot go on wandering aimlessly forever. Sooner or later, he will come back. We must find the courage to no longer fear the truth. This courage comes to us in silence. Silence is the courage of the truth, and truth the place of silence. In silence, the truth does not hurt me, she does not judge me, but only exhorts me to change: to return to the Father. 'Open your heart,' she tells me, 'and listen to my teaching.' Silence allows me to discover the truth, gently leads me to her and prepares my intelligence to welcome her, not as an unwelcome guest or an undesirable visitor, but as a great and noble lady…"

This fellow, as you have grasped, dear Polliodoro, evokes the spectre of silence. If men begin to be silent, we are utterly lost; not that we shall be lost and damned a second time, but that too few souls will share our perdition. In silence, they will understand great things — the most important things. We must prevent them from doing so. So full speed ahead with the indispensable distractions: social media for all, everywhere and at all times; uninterrupted internet connection, ever attached to the umbilical cord of the world, to the watchful eye that never lets you out of its sight; a television always turned on, chattering away!

Forgive this sudden outburst, but let us go back to reading that tantalising passage in the worn-out journal which, alas, did not end there, with the "great and noble lady" truth:

"…Without the truth my life is useless, my intelligence is vain, my love is empty. Nothing will have savour, because everything will be a figment of my imagination, a mere semblance of reality. If the truth is lacking, my existence will be a continuous struggle between the desire to know the meaning of things and the frustration of this desire, to which I voluntarily subject myself in order to be convinced that the truth does not really exist. I will live with this frustrated desire, the fruit of my will to power which, in reality, is rather a will to weakness. Without the truth, man is weak, he is like a reed blown by the wind of every hypothesis, of every idea. Without the truth, life is not worth living. The journey is too long and man falls back on his selfishness. We need to rediscover the truth of silence in order to understand the silence of truth, its apparent weakness and its being the constant object of derision and denial, its helplessness in the face of evil. Great things are weak but weak things are great, greater and stronger than the strong things of the world. Silence triumphs over selfishness. It allows me to overcome my will for maddening power: an ephemeral idyll which lasts a very short time and then leaves me abandoned and alone, at the mercy of myself. Silence is the harmony of truth that fascinates the will and reveals its necessity to the intellect. Truth is what it is, what things are, what I am. The truth simply is."

What do you think, my dear Polliodoro? A text to be censored and hurled into oblivion. That man, those men, no longer exist, yet from time to time they reappear on the world stage, which belongs to us, the theatre of propaganda against the truth. I will not hold my peace, but I will cry out from the depths of hell, "Those arrogant fools!" They do not know, or do not want to understand, that the truth does not exist, because, if it existed, it would be coercive, contrary to freedom of expression. It would be like levelling everyone at the same rank. And then everyone would become the same as everyone else and each one would be like all the others. Their truth crushes them under a degrading uniformity, ours on the contrary sets them free. I say "ours" because, after all, we citizens of the depths have our truth too. Everyone has his truth, even those who deny it. The latter do not want the truth, but only their truth, which fights against the objective truth. Just between us, and in absolute confidence, the existence of the truth cannot be absolutely denied. Denying the truth already implies, in itself, the statement of a principle which I want to uphold, and which, in order for it to be firmly maintained, I must acknowledge as true; otherwise, it would be utterly vain to make such a claim. I would be a lunatic who at once affirms and denies the same assertion, violating the law of non-contradiction, as well as the common sense of words. "Truth does not exist", for example, is a truth I affirm in order to deny the truth. But it is a truth. My subjective truth, but a truth nonetheless.

So it is a question of understanding whether or not the truth is *simply subjective*, or rather *not necessarily objective*; not what it is, in and of itself, regardless of my personal viewpoint and desires. The truth must be valid for everyone, not just for me, for it to be integrally, entirely true. Relativism is the weapon which we wield in order to oppose the discovery of the whole truth. It denies objective truth and flatters men with their truths, half-truths and half-lies, for if the truth is not whole, it soon becomes a lie.

Love thus gains the upper hand. Which love? "Love is love," they keep repeating. Every love, every one of its manifestations, even its betrayal. And this is more than logical: if there is no truth, there is no longer a measure of true love. Even the contradiction of love is love as long as it is free, as long as it is desired deep down. "Polyamory", my dear Polliodoro, is the final outcome of this modernity which you mentioned. Desire imposes itself at the expense of truth. Freedom grows out of all proportion and becomes destructive. Then along comes fear and society becomes a land of solitary beings who no longer know where they are going, why they are there or what they should do.

Do you realise now that truth is the problem? Fortunately, however, most of our patients — modern, post-modern and post-Christian — have renounced it in the name of freedom. We will continue to repeat to them this slogan for a better world:

"The truth prevents you from being yourself, limits you, enslaves you; it is rigidly fixed on the things that are and cannot be otherwise; it prevents you from being spontaneous and living your life. Take back your life, which is yours and no one else's. Enjoy your freedom to the full."

Before leaving you to your own reflections, dear Polliodoro, I would like to point out one last fact to keep in mind. If the truth does not exist, only my truth exists. This can be the denial of the truth in principle, but also much more; it is an interpretation of the truth. Everything is resolved in a hermeneutical problem. If the truth doesn't exist, only its interpretation exists: its varied understanding by the subject who seeks to understand a rapidly changing reality. In short, there is only one truth which is valid for everyone: the need to interpret the truth and dilute it according to the times and fashions of thought. And so everything slips away, everything changes, everything flows. Who will save them?

What is quite noteworthy is that the intrepid champions of freedom of conscience are now enemies of freedom of thought and speech. You are free to do and to say whatever suits your fancy, with one noteworthy exception: you may not speak the truth. When it comes to issues which we are now accustomed to referring to as "sensitive" — abortion, euthanasia, the undermining of marriage between a man and a woman and the family founded on this, etc. — they turn a deaf ear or even try to silence the speaker by depriving him of the right to speak or mocking him as a fundamentalist.

Freedom, my dear Polliodoro, is not the solution. Today two freedoms are in conflict: that of telling the truth and that of telling a half-truth made to one's own measure. This conflict exists because of a capital vice (please pardon the expression, I have the highest regard for all vices and consider them, in accordance with our long tradition, to be our main means of seduction): love of freedom over love of truth. Either they go together or else there is no love and no freedom. The champions of the freedom not to tell the truth are simply enemies of freedom, but friends of ours.

With my warmest regards, dear Polliodoro, I recommend that you be more prudent in future. Dare to do a bit less than your freedom of initiative and entrepreneurial spirit inspire you to do. Cheerio.

Your most affectionate mentor from the depths,

Arcibaldo

XIII.
The divine Prisoner

Dear Polliodoro,

I'm getting back to you after a very brief interlude. In my last letter I forgot to return to a point you mentioned in your eloquent though unsolicited assessment, which displayed a shadow of insubordination. You all of a sudden decided to take up pen and paper and write to me with an update on the doings of your patients and how you yourself view various events in the history of mankind. You sent me your opinion about the causes of the division that persists between them, but whose roots go deeper than their current quibbles. You depicted them as divisive people *per se* and not *per accidens* — I beg your pardon, I am always forgetting that this blessed *latinorum* is not yet completely familiar to you, but it is high time that you learned by heart a few of its rules in order to better understand how they speak, or how those patients of yours would speak if they were the least bit serious.

Per se and not *per accidens*: let me explain. By bringing about division among themselves, through a lot of deliberate decisions and a declaration of liberty for all, instead of simply suffering division as an unfortunate but necessary effect of their debates, they actually seek after division and relish it.

What I would now like to point out concerns your reflection on freedom severed from the truth. I cannot hide this from you either, though you should already be aware of it. There is at least one instance in which freedom rings untrue, revealing its weakness: a freedom to hate (more generally, we could say a freedom to do evil), which is quite useful for us, of course, and word about which we will continue to spread, like a sweet scent of genuine freedom.

He who hates is not free. But in spite of this, we must incite them to hate, to commit evil, so that they become free *with* us and *like* us. Their Master had warned them that whoever commits a sin becomes its slave and not its master (cf. Jn 8:34). Moreover, that wretched disciple, beloved of their Master (a real nuisance to us for many reasons, above all for taking unto him the Mother of our Enemy), wrote to the first Christians about unsavoury things which are difficult to digest:

> "He that committeth sin is of the devil: for the devil sinneth from the beginning. For this purpose, the Son of God appeared, that he might destroy the works of the devil." (1 Jn 3:8)

Most certainly. And we don't mind in the least! Indeed, we are proud of the fact, and stand ready to defy those who seek to destroy us. The will of the hardened sinner, entrenched in evil, becomes more and more bitter, callous, to the point of closing his heart to goodness and to love. If he doesn't have the strength of the Enemy to break free from that evil, from that hatred, it will drag him ever downward; it will even stick to his skin, envelop him like a coil that winds round his soul and body and will squeeze him, suffocate him, force him to do what he had never wanted to do. That hatred grows and devours him like a snake raised in his very bosom. This serpent appears to regenerate him, makes him feel as if he were his own master, but in fact it kills him. We, of the school of hatred, make sure that this feeling does not change, does not turn into forgiveness, into love, and thus leaves him forever in that same condition — in eternal hatred.

In fact, our hell is a condition that never ends, in which our freedom is lost forever, due to our having misused it. In this state, we cannot stop hating, and we are no longer free. And so on without end, in the name of freedom: of our freedom from the Enemy. This freedom that we invoke — the absence of God and the estrangement from Him — is no longer recognisable as freedom, but rather as necessity, as a wallowing in the dregs of the abyssal depths, where one is stuck in a condition that permanently binds the final choice made in life, for all eternity. Without the Enemy, the sole possibility is that of hating forever, of remaining in this condition of death, of being suffocated by an evil willed, flaunted, praised and glorified to the bitter end. Alas, freedom, without being free to avoid doing evil and to be liberated from evil, is no freedom at all. It is the suicide of freedom, it is its death knell, which we of the school of freedom from God eagerly and willingly propagate. We taught it to their progenitors, and ever since then, in a wily way, we have been luring everyone into the same trap. They believe they are free, but without being so, without the essence of freedom, which is the freedom to love, to do good. They are not capable of perceiving that only in the good is man free, because it is the good that sets him free.

At this point I find myself forced to give a counter-testimony and preach to you against our deep-seated convictions. The good does not force itself upon others, it neither usurps nor infringes on the rights of others. It only gives, hopes, offers itself, loves without expecting to be loved in return. It is perfect, gratuitous fulfilment, the eternal youthfulness of freedom. True goodness is accomplished by loving, without taking into account any evil received in return. *"Dilige et quod vis fac,"* wrote their Augustine, commenting on the first letter of that beloved disciple who is so unpalatable to us. Initially, the bishop of Hippo, overwhelmed by his weakness in resisting evil, devoured by deceptive and disordered passions, had plunged headlong into the goods of this world; into those things that are good because they participate in a goodness that they do not find in themselves but only in the One who is the Good — our Archenemy. Then regrettably, his conscience was pricked, the Enemy's good prevailed, and his eyes were opened. He began to love in truth by loving the truth, his Creator and Redeemer. And so, he could proclaim what I have just quoted to you in Latin: "Love and do what you will". To which he immediately added, "if you are silent, be silent for love's sake; if you speak, speak for love's sake; if you correct an erring soul, do so for love's sake; if you forgive, forgive for love's sake.

May the source of love be in you, because from this source only good can pour forth."

As if to say, by way of paraphrase, that only in true love, in the good, are you free and so able to become eternal; or to put it another way, love the good and thus you are free, because from the love of the good can only derive the goodness of love. This, in a nutshell, is the teaching of his master Plato, who, in the *Symposium* (on the nature of love) had said that "love is the desire for the perpetual possession of the good". In love there is the immortality of beauty and of goodness, because love itself is the desire for immortal and divine beauty that gives goodness. If you are not convinced, let me quote you a passage from the *Symposium*:

> "If, as we have agreed, the finality of love is the perpetual possession of the good, it necessarily follows that love must desire immortality along with the good, and this line of reasoning inevitably leads us to the conclusion that love is the love of immortality and of goodness."

I must confess to you, dear Polliodoro, that reading and rereading these words made me feel a momentary twinge of remorse that we are no longer capable of this. Every now and then, I can't help thinking about this and it sickens me that we can no longer turn back, that we are no longer capable of loving. Within their ranks, some have tried to liberate us from this suffering that will grip us forever, by trying to find a possible theological solution. They have opined that, in the end times, there will be an *apocatastasis*, a restoration of all things, through which even our Father of the depths, the devil, with all of his allies, will be able to be reconciled with the Enemy. Vanity of vanities! It is against Revelation, which teaches the existence of an eternal hell. And anyway, our pride prevents this reconciliation, otherwise it would be nothing more than a petty, piddling pride.

Yet I cannot deny to you that, deep down, a perpetual frustration urges all of us to make others also lose the possibility of loving and thus of being free in the good. But let us not wallow in self-pity, for our time is running out. We must find a way for many — for countless numbers of them — to forget this love and thus the good and, finally the truth of their freedom. They must know neither Plato nor Augustine, and above all, they must not know the Enemy.

Enough of these crocodile tears! I've devised another action plan. We must keep them away from the source of this love, from the Tabernacle. Do you want to know how we'll do it? We will proceed step by step. First we'll hide all the books and saints inciting love for the Blessed Sacrament of the altar; in this way their Eucharistic devotion will grow cold. How will we go about this? Certainly not by going around all the seminaries, convents, monasteries and parishes looting the libraries, stacking books in a huge pile and then destroying them in a late-night bonfire, nor by taking them to a second-hand bookshop and selling them cheap. That would be a waste of precious time, and besides, as you know, they often take care of this themselves. We will, however, try to convince them that these books and saints belong to times gone by, and that nowadays there are other more important and more pastoral things to think about. There is, as it were, a yawning chasm between the time of these ancient, rigorist and self-absorbed saints, and today, and this gap must not be filled by the saints themselves, nor their works, but by us — by an alternative way of thinking.

For instance, how could anyone today tolerate that book by a fanatical lover of Jesus in the Blessed Sacrament, a certain Alphonsus Maria of Liguori, who lived centuries ago and who wrote, for the devout and the pious of his day, that unbearable masterpiece entitled *Visits to the Blessed Sacrament and the Blessed Virgin Mary*? Not only did that rigid saint write this bestselling book, along with countless others, for the sole purpose of leading souls to his Jesus (just think, he wrote 111 works, with 21,000 editions in 70 languages, not to mention the composition of famous songs, musical texts, poems, paintings!) but he himself was forever captivated by his Eucharistic Jesus. In search of the path he must follow to put himself at the total service of the Enemy, he abandoned a brilliant legal career; and, in addition to daily Mass, and Communion several times a week, the Eucharistic presence would make him abandon not only the courtrooms but theatres, games, hunting and social gatherings as well. This irresistible presence drew him daily, every evening, to visit the Blessed Sacrament and the Blessed Virgin. He always had his eyes fixed on the monstrance, all-absorbed and permeated by the mystery that he adored, to the point that he failed to realise that his wig had slipped halfway off his head. His faith and devotion when still a layman aroused not only admiration but also bewilderment, especially on the part of priests, however devout they were.

Throughout his life he took care to adorn his beloved Prisoner with the most beautiful flowers from among the southern flora. He procured the rarest seeds and went to gather colourful flowers of varied beauty, in order to adorn the Tabernacles of the neighbouring convents. He envied the flowers, creatures of a rare beauty and innocent splendour, because they could stay day and night beside his beloved in the Tabernacle. He even wrote a spiritual canticle in which he praised the flowers. Take a look at this amorous extravagance:

> "O flowers, o happy flowers, which day and night
> So near to my own Jesus silent stay,
> And never leave Him, till before His sight,
> At length your life in fragrance fades away.
>
> "Could I, too, always make my dwelling-place
> In that dear spot to which your charms you lend,
> Oh, what a blessed lot were mine! what grace,
> Close to my truest Life, my life to end!"

He felt a certain regret seeing all those Christians making the pilgrimage to Jerusalem, feeling strong sentiments of devotion while visiting those blessed places: the stable where the divine Babe was born, the praetorium where He was scourged, Calvary where He was crucified and the tomb where He was buried. Yet, how much livelier should be the desire to visit the Tabernacle in the churches, where Jesus resides in person in the Blessed Sacrament? Many of them forgot this in those times also. There is even a prayer that accompanies each visit to the Blessed Sacrament, his act of spiritual communion:

> "My Jesus, I believe that you are present in the most Blessed Sacrament. I love You above all things and I desire to receive You into my soul. Since I cannot now receive You sacramentally, come at least spiritually into my heart. (Pause) I embrace You as if You were already there, and unite myself wholly to You. Never permit me to be separated from You."

We have to make sure that this prayer disappears completely. And along with it, the book of *Visits* and the saint himself. Too much trouble, but besides, far too much pious devotionalism, showing little socio-pastoral tact for evangelising the world by letting the world evangelise them, don't you think? Poor old man, all hunched to one side, with his head almost resting on his shoulder, and yet he kept on praying: he still wanted to be brought before the altar to speak with his Beloved. Enough of these childish devotions! We will never forgive that man for having lived during the Enlightenment without letting himself be enlightened. On the contrary, he tried to smother those lights of ours and overshadow them with the light of his Jesus. Sadly enough, he succeeded.

But this is not the only trick we have up our sleeve in order to lure them away from the Tabernacle. That is just the first step. The next will be to convince them that, with the discovery of the common priesthood of the faithful, such faithful must do much more than remain on their knees at the foot of the Tabernacle. They must be more active, more committed to the liturgy, mixing themselves with the priests and deacons, without being either one or the other. They will be a cross between the clerical and the lay state. We could call them clerical-laity, who rise above a lowbrow popular culture — with all due respect to their offspring, who have no idea whether or not these men seen at the altar, acting as an alternative power, half-priest and fully empowered layperson, are still their natural fathers! Then they have to get out of the churches and onto the streets, towards the peripheries of existence (not to the ends of the earth), bringing social justice to everyone. They will do charity work without charity, without their Jesus. Well now, doesn't that sound like a good idea to you?

And then there is the final step, which must be taken cautiously but decisively, without breaking with the preceding one. Little by little, we will close the churches. They will be so busy going out into the streets and talking to their neighbours that they won't have any more time to stay in church. And then what good are all their churches (which should in truth be called theatres, amphitheatres, dining rooms, recreation halls, film clubs and bars)? If ever they do happen to be open, one will need a state-of-the-art satellite navigator to identify the remote nook where the Blessed Sacrament has been hidden away. Their Jesus is an exile in

His own Church! We will convince them to abandon the churches and thus they will desert their divine Prisoner. Then will come the complete closure: neither a lighted lamp to indicate His presence nor a candle to illuminate the darkness of the night. Not even a flower to decorate the altar. And there He will remain, waiting patiently, even in the pitch darkness, "dumb as a lamb before his shearer" (Is 53:7), silent before those who tear His beard and spit in His face. He is there, a prisoner, because this is how love manifests itself. This is Love.

Have you caught my drift? We've still got to give our all to make sure the Tabernacle is increasingly hidden and the divine Prisoner an unwelcome guest, a stranger in His own home. If they discovered that it is love that has made a prisoner of Him, they would also understand what freedom is, which is genuine when one is able to renounce it for the sake of love. This is its maximum manifestation and its ultimate fulfilment.

To work then, dear Polliodoro, without letting ourselves be persuaded by winds of contrary doctrine and without shedding tears. I send you now my warmest wishes and recommend that you give free reign to your imagination and enterprising spirit. You will see to it that the freedom to be and to love continues to be occluded, and thus freedom will be no more.

From the depths below, your most affectionate mentor,

Arcibaldo

XIV.
A toast to us

Dear Polliodoro,

Well, this is it. I dare say we can be quite satisfied with our work. I am particularly pleased to learn that, despite your obstinacy and doctrinal difficulties, and though you are wont to turn up your nose from time to time, you did quite a fine job. Ideas always do the trick and, as you've seen, we've got quite a few to sell which our patients are always willing to buy.

I would like to acquaint you with a revealing fact about a certain mentality. The other day, while on my evening stroll to get some fresh air after an intense day of labour in sweltering heat, I happened upon a strange sight — like a scene from a dramatic film, set in past times, long since vanished from the face of the earth, but in fact a contemporary scene. It was a heartfelt and heated discussion between a priest and a pious lady who was asking the reverend father for something quite improper. It touched a nerve with both.

He appeared to be in his mid-sixties, with well-groomed hair lacquered with gel, parted down the middle as if to show, even on his head, "a before and an after". He was decked out in beige trousers that fell perfectly on his well-polished shoes, and a short-sleeved shirt, unbuttoned just enough to reveal abundant chest hair. He had an Italian-sounding nickname, *Pino*, and rigidly refused the title of "Father" (actually, he was called Pinuccio by his closest collaborators).

She was a devout woman named Delphine, quite a bit younger in age; if my eyes did not deceive me, I would say she must have been twenty years younger than him. She was prim, proper and modestly dressed, as was surely her custom when in a sacred place, though her youthfulness and grace could have prompted some laxity in this area. I tuned in, and savouring what I heard, listened to their entire discussion.

"Is there a need for conversion to become a Christian?" asked the lady. They were in the sacristy after Mass, with young female altar servers and older ladies in miniskirts who had distributed the Eucharist.

"It is merely a matter of understanding what conversion means," replied the priest, with a hermeneutical accent. "If it is a question of finding oneself, of turning back to oneself after having lost and perhaps buried oneself under heaps of little devotional books, then yes: conversion is necessary, as God intended us to be thus. If, on the other hand, conversion means renouncing oneself in order to find the fullness of God once again in the emptiness of oneself, then no: this has the stench of an outdated theology. It is like the pious chanting of lengthy prayers, which makes you content with having gorged yourself on holy exclamations, in the utter void of your own thoughts and in the absence of your own initiative. God does not want to fill our void. He has made us with all that is necessary for us to fulfil our needs, to be sufficient unto ourselves. It is simply a question of rediscovering what is our own, what really matters. God has no time to waste filling us with all sorts of things whilst leaving us without what is truly necessary: our being, here and now, at the service of the world. Isn't it being that counts? Let's live our existence to the full, to the core. Let's simply be."

Those words were at once engraved in her mind. "Being, here and now … *to the core*." But I could see that, the more the lady reflected, the more she began to be disdainful, clearly desiring to voice her disagreement. I sensed that she was close to bursting. But she restrained herself.

"And yet, Father," replied Delphine, who tried to put aside her puzzlement and pursue the subject with a more peaceful reflection, "I believe that one is not born to live just for oneself and for oneself alone. This would not succeed in any case, because life always requires another, a relationship."

"I agree with you," replied the priest, "but please, call me Pino, so we can simplify the approach. I am not saying that man is made to live just for himself, but that he cannot find God or others except to the extent that he turns to himself, to his person, the centre of his existence, which is the very reason why he was willed by God in the first place."

"Forgive me … Father," replied Delphine, who had tried her best to say *Pino*, "but this way of speaking sounds rather novel to me. How could man possibly find God and others simply by rediscovering himself? Doesn't the Catechism teach us, and isn't it true, that to the extent that we become close to God, we find ourselves and love others too? Otherwise, our love for others would be only human; just our feelings and nothing more."

With growing confidence, she had the presence of mind to follow with a quote from Saint Augustine (one that is best forgotten): "You only love your friend truly when you love God in your friend, either because God is in him, or in order that God may be in him. This is true love: if we love for any other reason, what we feel is more akin to hatred than to love."

It seemed she had never spoken out like this before. Fortunately, our Pino was there to parry the blow and to calm the spirits of those in the sacristy who, by this point, were listening with a great desire to participate in this post-catechetical theological discussion.

"Delphine," replied the priest, "I naturally have great respect for Augustine of Hippo, but his sermons must be contextualised. That sermon you were quoting is one I know almost by heart since, in the seminary, they instilled it into our minds to the point of sheer boredom: it's number 336. This sermon was given for the dedication of a church, of which, most likely, he was not the consecrating bishop, as was to be the case in the following sermon; as you know, a church is certainly not dedicated every month. I don't mean to deny the love of God, but to affirm the centrality of the human person, this centrality taking precedence over God and in a phenomenological way, that is, starting from the person himself. If you don't know man, you don't know God. Saint Augustine said this as well."

"So, Father," Delphine replied immediately, "is it no longer true that man was created in the image and likeness of God? And that God is the first principle?"

"I do not deny that God is the first principle," replied Father Pino, surrounded by an assembly that was now hanging on every word coming from his lips. The sacristy seemed to be shrinking so that it too could huddle around the parish priest. "On the image and likeness, however, I would like to say a few more words. Of course, man is an image bearing resemblance to God. But since that image is in man and that man is the image of God, this blessed image no longer has any reason to seek a meaning outside itself, it does not point to anything else beyond itself: it is man. It is an image that is in a certain sense anthropomorphised. It remains here, in this world. It does not fly away and take to the skies, it does not disperse, nor does it claim to ascend to heaven-knows-where. God has disposed that man may participate in his identity, as an intelligent and free being, but it is now time for man to play His own role in history. If we expected a God who rescues the infirm, who bails humanity out of the fine mess it's in, we would rather have made God in the image and likeness of man. This is decidedly not what we want. On the contrary, we want man to be this image which is carved in Him. We want man to join in the game now. For far too long the Church has insisted on such concepts as 'relationship with God', 'grace' understood as a 'supernatural bond', 'conversion', and 'return to God'. It is high time for us to dust off the phenomenological concept, like a wonderful piece of antique furniture that has accumulated a lot of dust over time. It is time to restore man's dignity."

Delphine listened with a dumbfounded, almost ashen face. She didn't know if that sacristy preacher was trying to put her faith to the test or if he was improvising a panegyric to humanity. I was watching the scene very closely, dear Polliodoro, and was thoroughly enjoying myself. From time to time, I noticed a more theoretical accent from our Pinuccio, so that his arguments cut off every one of the pious lady's words before they could even be voiced, deadening their impact and defusing their power, even before they could see the light of day. Delphine was utterly exhausted. She would have liked to throw in the towel, to leave the sacristy. Though still shuddering from the shock, she was suddenly seized by a spiritual jolt, and vehemently replied:

"Dear Father, it seems to me that all this talk is full of anthropocentrism, masked by good intentions. But it saves no one. It does not make humanity new; on the contrary, it leaves humanity wallowing in its misery. We Christians are no longer able to speak to the world because, at this point, we are no longer capable of distinguishing ourselves from it. The world has entered the Church but the Church is still struggling to penetrate the world. Despite your openness and overtures to the world, the world continues to hate us.

Christians are persecuted in the world because they are guilty of following a Crucified God. The Cross is still a scandal. I see that you are ashamed of the Cross. Is there no longer any faith left? Has it simply vanished into thin air?"

"My dear Delphine," continued Father Pino, "how completely mistaken you are. It is only thanks to this bold leap of novelty that we will be able to build bridges rather than walls, to create bonds of brotherhood between men in the name of their own selves and not in the name of divisive ideologies — be they religious or political, social or economic. Engrave this deeply into your memory: ideologies divide, whereas love for man unites and fulfils our longing for fraternity. Love for man and for humanity, of which he is a microcosm and a very high expression. This is our mission: 'the event of God's absolute and forgiving self-communication'."

All were seized with great reverence upon hearing those words. We dwellers of the infernal depths could not have put it better ourselves. Suddenly, in the atmosphere of smug, self-satisfied silence that enveloped the room, the sacristan appeared at the door. A disciple of the parish priest and of these ideas of his, she was an elderly lady, but quite distinguished and genteel; one of those who had experienced to the very marrow of her bones that fateful "before and after" that her dear Pinuccio wore sculpted in his hair. She knew that a dispute had been heating up on a central point of today's faith and the mission of the Church. She always kept her ear to the ground, making sure she did not miss out on anything that was being said, so as to keep everything well under control. She had always been very much in favour of moving ahead, of progress; certainly not to dilute the faith, as she repeatedly said, but to cause a leap of joy forward, on the part of those like herself for whom, partly because of their age, partly because of their health issues, that giant leap might end up being somewhat of a flop.

With some degree of affectation, after the manner of an expert in all things ecclesiastical, she approached the group and showed her beloved Pinuccio the latest issue of a publication that updated the clergy on the latest news regarding pastoral life. A remarkable headline stood out in big bold letters: "We are all brothers". And this was accompanied by a slightly faded image of the Pope giving a blessing.

"Now take a look at this! What do you think?" exclaimed the faithful sacristan, with a menacing look in Delphine's eyes that seemed to say, "The question's been settled once and for all. The debate is over. Long live Pinuccio and his paradigm shift, now officially confirmed."

Father Pino, who had only heard a brief news item on the radio concerning the papal encyclical on universal brotherhood, wanted to flip through some excerpts from it, quoted in that magazine. He stumbled upon this passage, almost a synthesis of the whole text. He read it aloud for everyone:

"Let us dream, then, as a single human family, as fellow travellers sharing the same flesh, as children of the same earth, which is our common home, each of us bringing the richness of his or her beliefs and convictions, each of us with his or her own voice, brothers and sisters all!"

He then read another, in which the Pope quoted a film in which he himself had been the protagonist:

"A journey of peace is possible between religions. Its point of departure must be God's way of seeing things. 'God does not see with his eyes; God sees with his heart. And God's love is the same for everyone, regardless of religion. Even if they are atheists, his love is the same. When the last day comes, and there is sufficient light to see things as they really are, we are going to find ourselves quite surprised!'"

As Father Pino continued reading, his voice grew softer, to the point that he seemed to have forgotten those present. These were the prerequisites for finally being able to build a new humanism, after the secular post-humanism imposed by a rather Jacobin intellectual trend — but starting afresh, from a love that no longer admits of distinctions. God's love is free and universal, it embraces man as such, and no longer demands that he be reborn as a son in the Son. Furthermore, the question of whether God has a Son, and whether this Son is God, is not such a simple question to answer, nor such an easy thing to affirm. Indeed, affirming such a thing would be divisive. So much research on the historical Jesus has come to naught, so many questions have remained unanswered, whereas the same question always remains there on the surface, like salt spray swallowed while swimming in a stormy sea. Is Jesus *really* the Son of God? God only knows! Man can never really be sure, because the information he possesses is not historical and, even if it were, it is not reliable. Mission accomplished, my dear Polliodoro!

Delphine decided not to speak anymore. I could see her moving her lips almost as if she were talking to someone invisible. Her expression dimmed; she was dismal indeed. A few tears even ran down her cheeks. What more could she possibly add? *Roma locuta est, causa soluta est* — "Rome has spoken, the case is closed". This verdict struck down her faith. Father Pino and his sacristan were right. So she resigned herself and decided to leave the sacristy in silence, perhaps to return some other time, when there was less frenzied cheering and chanting from the stadium. But she didn't stop going to church, to remain alone in front of the Tabernacle.

My dear Polliodoro, I congratulate you heartily on the excellent work you've accomplished. We have achieved fine results, which would have been unthinkable in times gone by. A new areligious humanism is upon them. Despite more than one warning about a sly and insidious Antichrist presenting himself as the greatest benefactor of humanity, a philanthropist who unites everyone in his own name — without and against the Enemy — they are now letting their guard down. An Antichristic time is upon them, its outline is already perceptible on the horizon, without much fanfare and with their full consent. In an Antichristic time, an anti-Church is also being born which is the opposite of the

Church and of the faith. Not man's faith in God, but God's faith in man. No longer the Mystical Body of Christ that unites all men in grace, saving them from eternal ruin, but a fraternal union of all men that forms the mystical body of man, with only one religion: love. Its aim is to create a better, more equitable and more fraternal world, with fewer taxes and more jobs for all. Especially without private property, the last natural deterrent that safeguards the uniqueness and dignity of man, distinguishing him from everyone else.

A toast to a job well done! But be careful. Remain vigilant. The Enemy never rests, and you never know, He just might play a dirty trick on us. Love thus understood ultimately comes to an end, as has already happened so many times over. *Homo homini lupus* — "Man is a wolf to other men". This realisation might just make a comeback and do damage to our vineyard as, if one day they find themselves without this love of ours, they just might seek after something else.

So, it's good-bye for now, but don't you worry, we'll be seeing each other again soon. But for the moment, let's just be at ease, and savour this fine success of ours.

Your very affectionate mentor,

Arcibaldo